His Rogue Bear

Weres & Witches of Silver Lake
Book 11

Vella Day

One murder. One lost memory. Two mates trying not to die.

Werebear Blair Murdoch doesn't think things can get any worse. Boy, is she wrong. While she struggles to find her bear, she has to deal with a super hot werewolf, Ronan Laramie, who insists on sticking around. The problem is that she can't remember a damn thing about a murder she's supposed to have committed. Talk about going from bad to worst.

Ronan considers his assignment to protect Blair good fortune until he finds out that he has to battle with his wolf to keep from ravishing her every second of every day. Then catastrophe strikes, and Ronan has no choice but to prepare for battle.

Can these two star-crossed lovers live long enough to fulfill their fantasy life, or will a power great than they've ever known rip them apart?

Beneath the calm and shimmering surface lie intrigue, power, magic, and danger.
Welcome to Silver Lake—where appearances can be deceiving, and what you see isn't truly what lies below.

Chapter One

B LAIR MURDOCH'S THOUGHTS were speeding down all the wrong roads, hurdling past every blockade, and then tumbling into a tangled mess. Her physical therapy patients claimed she was the epitome of calm, but right now, she felt as if an opaque swath of gauze had wrapped itself around her mind, suffocating all coherent thoughts. Maybe her friend Ainsley was right. She needed to take a few days off from work.

Stabbing the key into her apartment front door, Blair twisted it, and shoved it open. The intense July heat was probably the culprit for her disorientation. That or something at work had done a number on her. Only what?

As soon as she stepped inside, Blair lowered the thermostat then tossed her keys and purse on the dining room table, feeling slightly better with the rush of cooler air. Her bright red sofa and the fun artwork on the walls usually boosted her spirits after a long day of work, but nothing short of a glass of white wine would perk her up tonight.

Stepping around the table to grab a bottle from the wine rack, she leaned over and froze. What the hell? A colorful mosaic of reddish brown was sprayed across her white work shirt.

Well shit. She tried to brush off the sprinkling of color, hoping it was some kind of powder, but nothing happened. As she examined the stain closer, her breath refused to expel. Holy fuck, it was dried blood. Forgetting all about her wine, she rushed to the bathroom to find the source.

One look in the mirror and she freaked. Besides the swath of color on her shirt, her auburn hair was mussed, faint bruising appeared on her upper arms, and her chin and cheek had speckles of dried blood that resembled an allergic reaction. As acid attacked her stomach with a vengeance, bile clawed its way up her throat. How had this happened? She would have remembered injuring herself, only nothing came to mind.

Blair lifted her shirt, and only after she found no evidence of an injury did that pent up breath she'd been holding sprint out. Only a few flecks dotted her white bra, implying the blood was someone else's. Only where had it come from? She'd left work ten minutes ago and driven straight home. From the lack of smearing, she hadn't rubbed up against anything. There was no way liquid could have flown in her window on the drive home. She always kept the air on this time of year.

Think! She remembered saying goodbye to Eve at the receptionist's desk, who said nothing about Blair looking like a train wreck. She then left by the side door that led to the alley. Blair tried to picture walking past the dumpster to the parking lot in back and then climbing into her car, but that image refused to materialize. The only thing she recalled was putting the key in the front door lock a few seconds ago.

So what had transpired in between leaving work and arriving home? Concentrate! Had there been a lot of annoying traffic on the drive home, or had luck been on her side, and she'd flown down the streets? Damn. She couldn't even dredge up one single memory, but that didn't mean she'd stop trying.

Blair mentally snapped her fingers. Maybe she'd stopped to help a car wreck victim. That would explain where the blood came from. The trauma might have caused her to block out the horrible event. Yeah, that was it.

Or was it? She'd witnessed some pretty horrific injuries in her line of work and had never been squeamish before.

Sure, she'd been stressed out these last few weeks but not enough to cause her to forget something like being doused with what looked like arterial spray.

As much as she wanted to rip off her white uniform shirt and jump in the shower, her detective brother had trained her not to tamper with evidence—assuming that was what it was.

Most likely, her imagination had tumbled down the wrong rabbit hole, and the reddish brown coloring wasn't even blood. A trickle of relief shot through her at that thought. To test her theory, she poured a bit of hydrogen peroxide on one spot. When it bubbled up white, the ramification nearly strangled her. It was blood. Only whose?

Scared, yet determined to get to the bottom of this, Blair strode back to the living room and snatched her phone from her purse to call Kalan. Hopefully, he wasn't on some case for the sheriff's department and not able to be reached. When on stakeout, he often turned off the ringer. If anyone knew of an accident, it would be him.

She dialed his number, and he answered on the second ring. "Hey, Blair."

She didn't detect any undue stress in his voice, meaning he might not have heard of the supposed disaster. Knowing help was near, relief danced through her veins. Pressing the phone close to her ear, she edged her way over to the sofa and dropped down. "Thank goddess I got a hold of you. I think something bad has happened."

"What is it?"

"I don't know."

"What do you mean you don't know?"

She told him about the blood on her shirt and face. With each word uttered, her voice leaped upward, and a rush of panic flooded her system once more.

"Calm down," Kalan said. "You said you witnessed a car accident?"

"No. I said the blood might have come from someone in a car

accident, but I can't be sure."

"What is the last thing you remember?"

Logic was Kalan's middle name. It was why he made a great Beta to the Clan as well as a detective. "Calling you."

"No, I mean before that. After you left work."

"I remember nothing."

"Are you sure a patient didn't bleed on you?" he asked.

She was a physical therapist, not a nurse. "Yes, I'm sure." Her damn voice trembled.

"Are you okay though?"

Was he kidding? "No, I'm not okay. I can't remember a damn thing. What if I hit someone with my car and severely injured them?" That was a reach, but she needed him to take her seriously.

"Was your car in an accident?"

"I don't know." Blair stood and peered out the window. Her blue Corolla appeared unscathed. "I mean no."

"Blair, I'm sure there is a logical explanation. What worries me is that you can't remember anything."

"Tell me about it."

"Here's what we'll do. Lock your doors, and don't wash up or anything," her brother commanded. A drawer closed, and then his keys jangled. "I'm on my way. Don't worry. We'll figure it out. Everything will be okay."

"You don't know that," she blurted.

"Blair. Please. Do as I say."

"Fine," she said, though her chin was wobbling. At least Kalan hadn't assumed she'd committed some terrible crime.

As soon as her brother disconnected, Blair sat down and closed her eyes, forcing herself to think—only nothing came to mind. After searching for some trigger to help with her memory, she opened her eyes wide. Oh, crap. She'd forgotten to lock her front door, something she normally did as soon as she stepped inside her apartment. She had clearly angered some goddess today.

Once she took care of securing her apartment, she poured that glass of wine that she now needed desperately.

Wait a minute.

Had Kalan told her to lock up because he believed someone was after her, or was he being his usual cautious self? His words of wisdom climbed into her mind and took root. He always preached never to jump to conclusions. She'd have to ask him when he arrived.

By the time her big brother knocked on her door, she'd bitten two of her fingernails down to the quick. Setting her drink down, she rushed to answer it. After checking that it was Kalan, she opened up, but because her hands were shaking, she hid them behind her back.

Kalan stepped inside and ran his gaze up and down her body. "My goddess, Blair—you weren't kidding," he said as he led her over to the sofa.

She was right. She did look bad. "Can I get you some tea or a glass of wine?" she asked, wanting things to be normal again.

"No, I'm good. Sit down and tell me everything."

"I already told you everything."

"Okay. Let's start at the beginning. What time did you leave work?" Kalan asked.

Hadn't she told him that already? Blair would have appreciated some sympathy first, but Kalan was a cop. "At the same time I always leave—five o'clock."

"It's six now. What happened between then—?"

As she grappled with his claim of what time it was, her pulse galloped. "Six? It can't be! I just got home."

Kalan studied her then pulled out his phone from his top pocket and showed her the time. "Are you saying you lost track of time too?"

She didn't know what she was saying. "I, ah, left work at five and arrived home a few minutes ago. At least it seemed like only minutes."

"But you can't remember what happened in between?"

"No."

Kalan tapped his fingers on his knee. "Could someone have

drugged you? That might explain the time and memory loss."

"No!" she practically shouted. "I would have remembered that."

Kalan stabbed a hand through his hair. "Are you sure?"

Her back slumped. "No, I'm not sure of anything anymore."

He rubbed her shoulder. "How about coming down to the station so we can check you out? If there are drugs in your system, don't you want to know? It could explain a lot of things."

It was a fact that women who had unknowingly been given Rohypnol—the date rape drug—weren't even aware of it later on. The problem with that scenario was that she hadn't had anything to drink, or so she believed.

Before she could agree to anything, his cell rang, and he lifted a finger. "Murdoch. I'm at Blair's house, why? She had an…incident. When? Behind the Wellness Center? Damn. Sure. I'll be right there."

At the mention of her place of work, her heart plummeted. Kalan disconnected, but he didn't make eye contact.

"What happened?" she asked, acid charging up her throat.

"A dead body was found in the alley behind your work."

If she'd been upset before, it didn't compare to the head pounding and the tightness in her chest she was experiencing right now. Blair had to cover her mouth to keep from throwing up. "Do you think I did this?"

"It doesn't matter what I believe, but I'm afraid that I'll have to take you in."

"You're arresting me?" she croaked.

Kalan let out a breath. "No, but we need to process you to eliminate any reasonable doubt. There's a big difference. We need to collect the evidence first." He nodded to her shirt. "Let's hope the blood didn't come from the victim, though even if it did, it doesn't mean you harmed him. Maybe you were trying to help."

Yes, that was it. She was trying to help. "Why would the victim still be in the alley? Wouldn't I have called for help? The coroner would have taken him away already."

"Let's not jump to conclusions."

While she prided herself on being strong, tears welled in her eyes. Only once before in her life had she been this devastated, and she never wanted to repeat that mental torture again.

Blair stood. "Do you mind if I take a clean set of clothes with me? I promise I won't try to climb out the bedroom window and escape."

"Blair, please. I know you're innocent of any wrongdoing. You're a Murdoch."

She hadn't been the upstanding Murdoch everyone believed when she'd lived in Georgia. "Thanks. I'll only be a minute."

With a lead ball rattling around in her belly, she trudged to her bedroom where she gathered some fresh clothes and stuffed them in a small overnight bag. It shouldn't matter what she put on after the exam, but somehow her best black lace bra and matching panties would help her cope better. And because the sheriff's department was notoriously cold, she grabbed a sweater. For ease of changing, she picked out a pair of lightweight capris to go with her black sleeveless shirt.

A large inhale didn't help ease the pounding in her head or the riot going on in her stomach. Regardless of her emotional state, she needed to find some answers.

Chapter Two

B LAIR HAD LISTENED to Kalan tell stories about what went on at the sheriff's department many times, but she'd never imagined being processed would be so humiliating. Standing on a large sheet of paper while someone watched as you took off your clothes was not only embarrassing, it implied guilt. Then there was the hair brushing, the nail scrapings, and even worse was the pelvic exam to rule out rape.

Blair didn't want to think what prison would be like—invasive, taunting, and highly demoralizing. The only positive thing about the experience was that the person conducting the inspection was female, though Blair didn't want to think about who would be looking at the photos. As far as she could tell, there were no markings on her body other than the bruising on her upper arms, so hopefully there wasn't much to see.

"You can wash your hands and face in the sink over there. Then get dressed," the attendant said as she handed Blair a set of maroon scrubs.

"I brought something to change into." She nodded to the bag she'd placed on the chair. "My brother—Kalan Murdoch—said it was okay."

The attendant's eyes widened. "Then I'm sure it will be," she said. "I'll be back shortly.

So what was next? More questions she couldn't answer? Agonizing over the future wouldn't help her state of mind. Unfortunately, she couldn't help it. As she dressed, Blair wondered if they'd toss her in jail until the blood results came back, or would they let her go home until they knew more?

Trying to find the silver lining, Blair had to believe that Kalan would do whatever it took to make the second option happen.

What seemed like a lifetime later, someone knocked on the exam room and then pushed open the door. It was Kalan, and Blair sagged in relief. "So?" she asked, hoping his sallow complexion and sad eyes didn't indicate bad news.

"I'm afraid the blood on your shirt matches that of the deceased."

"What?" Her vision turned dark, forcing Blair to grasp the examination table to keep from collapsing. "How is that possible?"

Kalan held up a hand. "Having the blood on your shirt is circumstantial evidence. It doesn't mean you killed him."

"Am I in the clear then?" Blair didn't believe that for one moment.

Kalan pressed his lips together. "I'm afraid not. You also had gunshot residue on your hands."

Blair immediately lifted her shaking fingers to see if what he said was true. Only then did she remember that the fine granules would be invisible to the naked eye. Not to mention she'd washed her hands. "How is that possible? You don't think that I shot someone, do you?" Blood pulsed in her head as butterflies beat against her stomach.

"You shot something."

That was preposterous. "I don't even own a gun."

"I know, but gunshot residue doesn't just appear on your hands unless you fire a weapon."

The words swam around in her head, but she was having a hard time putting the pieces together. "Where would I have gotten a gun? Search my car and my house. You won't find one." Hysteria had taken root.

Kalan stepped closer and placed a gentle hand on her shoulder.

"Come with me."

"Where?" she snapped as her heart screamed for release.

"You need to call a lawyer."

"Are you arresting me?" This was a nightmare.

Kalan's lips thinned in a grimace. "I don't have a choice. You have the victim's blood on your shirt and GSR on your hands."

"I'm not guilty, or at least I don't think I am," Blair said. She had been so sure that all of this had been a mistake. Now she was beginning to doubt everything.

"We'll figure it out. Come on." Kalan escorted her down the hallway. When they arrived at Interrogation Room number 3, he pushed open the door.

"Why are we here?" Blair couldn't help but question everything.

"I'm hoping you'll remember something that will prove you were an innocent bystander." He didn't sound as if he believed her, and that shook her confidence to the core.

As if on autopilot, Blair stepped inside the dark, cold room. The small windowless area contained one plain brown table like the ones she'd eaten at in elementary school. Two chairs were pressed up against one side of the table while a lone chair sat across from them. Kalan motioned she take the single chair.

"I don't have a phone to call a lawyer," she said. "Can you call Jillian for me?" The lawyer's brother, Dalton, was Kalan's partner. Jillian was a white tiger shifter who also was a friend.

"Sure. I'm also going to call Judge Hollars to see if he can set bail. I don't want you to spend any time in jail."

Her hope soared. "Do you think he will do that?"

"The Murdoch name carries a lot of weight in this town."

To the shifter community maybe, but the humans had no idea they helped guide their Clan. "Thank you."

"Sit tight. It may be a while before I get ahold of him."

"I love you!"

"Love you back, and I promise I will do everything to find out what happened. Try not to worry." Kalan shot her a brief smile, but it didn't erase the worry on his face. As soon as he left, the monster of doubt poked out its ugly head, making her want to vomit and hide away forever—but she wouldn't. Blair Murdoch was a fighter.

RONAN LARAMIE STOOD in front of his boss' desk, disturbed by the unexpected and delightful news. "Are you sure Timothy Delahart is dead?"

Connor McKinnon leaned back in his chair. "Yes. I just spoke with Dalton Garner, Kalan's partner at the sheriff's department."

"How could a bullet kill a werewolf though?" Ronan had been shot a few times, but thankfully he'd never been hit in a vital spot. It was why his wolf had no trouble healing him.

"It must have been a clean shot to the throat."

"There goes that bounty." While the reward money would have come in handy, he was glad the drug dealing, human trafficker was off the streets. "Do we have any idea who killed him?"

"Nope, but Kalan and Dalton are on the case. They'll find him."

"I'm thinking it was a shifter. A human would have aimed for the heart."

"Makes sense. So far no witnesses have come forward, and until we get a copy of the autopsy, we won't know if there was any evidence of a mauling."

Ronan didn't know why he should care who killed the scum, but he didn't like loose ends.

Connor's cell rang, sending Ronan's contemplative mood running for cover.

His boss glanced at the phone. "It's Kalan. Maybe he's learned something," he said as he swiped a finger across the phone. "Yeah?" He listened for a good fifteen seconds. "No way! Why didn't you call me sooner?" Connor dragged a hand down his jaw looking as if he'd been told someone had died—someone important. "And Blair remembers nothing?"

Blair? Ronan's wolf awoke with a start. As much as he'd tried these past two weeks to deny that Blair Murdoch was his mate, as sure as he was sitting there in Connor's office, he knew that she was. He hadn't spoken to her since the party when Connor and his mate had announced their good news, but Ronan had thought of nothing else but her since then.

Connor asked Kalan a few more questions and then disconnected. His boss stabbed a hand through his hair, looking off to the side and saying nothing.

Ronan pulled out the chair in front of his desk and sat. "What happened?"

Connor blew out a breath. "Blair has been arrested for Delahart's murder."

He almost laughed, but his boss' serious nature stopped him. "That's ridiculous. Not only is Blair not a killer, she never would have had any dealings with Delahart. The man was a drug dealer and a human trafficker, to name a few of his less than pleasant occupations."

Connor held up a hand. "You don't have to convince me, but she had his blood on her shirt and GSR on her hand."

Ronan's pulse shot off at a gallop. There had to be an explanation. "What does Blair say happened?"

"She remembers nothing about the event."

"What do you mean?"

Connor shrugged. "She has a memory lapse during the time of his death."

"Did someone put a spell on her?"

"I was wondering the same thing. It was either that, or the trauma of seeing someone die caused the memory loss. I hope it's just a spell. At least that will wear off at some point."

"Maybe she was drugged."

"Preliminary tests showed she wasn't. If she experienced something traumatic, she might never recover. Blair is the sensitive type," Connor said.

Ronan's mind jumped to a dark place. "You don't think someone attacked or possibly raped her and she fought back, do you?" He could barely say that word. His nails sharpened, and hair sprouted on his face.

"Calm down."

Ronan's immediate and visceral reaction would be hard to explain if Connor questioned him. "I can't calm down."

"No, she wasn't raped. She was checked for that as well."

The air shot out of his lungs, and his nails and hair retracted. He then asked, "So now what?"

Connor studied him. "You seem unusually interested. I didn't realize you knew Blair that well."

"I don't, but I know what it's like to be accused of a crime you didn't commit."

"I get it."

"Do you think I should speak with her? I knew Timothy Delahart better than anyone. If Blair had any interaction with the man, I'd like to know what he said. It might help figure out who really did kill him." Ronan was grasping at straws.

"Let's wait and see what the judge says. Kalan is trying to set bail now."

Ronan didn't want to wait, but he would—for Blair's sake.

"WHAT DO YOU think happened?" Blair's lawyer, Jillian Garner asked.

Blair was tired of the same old questions. "I don't know how many times I have to say it; I don't remember anything! Nada." She hadn't meant to raise her voice. Her lawyer was only trying to help. "I'm sorry. Since the tests indicate I wasn't drugged, all I can come up with is that someone must have cursed me or something that suppressed my memory."

"It's a good theory. Do you remember any incantations, arm waving, burning candles?"

Now she wished she had paid better attention to what her

Wendayan friends had told her about spells. Her former roommate, Ainsley, had been no help since she hadn't embraced her shifter or Wendayan side during their school years. "No. No candles, no funky scents, nothing. I'd remember if I was put into a trance, right?"

"Spells don't always mean a trance. A capable black witch can do things to you that you aren't even aware are happening," Jillian said and then pressed her lips together in a sympathetic pose. "When you get out of here, maybe you should contact Ophelia. I've heard she can work wonders in reversing spells—or at least identifying who put the spell on you."

Blair had heard that too, but with her luck, the spell would be one that couldn't be broken. "I'll do that."

Jillian pushed back her chair. "I'll check with Kalan on the status of your release. Don't worry, we'll get it all straightened out."

The question Blair hadn't wanted to ask finally broke free like water pushing against a weak dam, and her body shook at the implication. "What if I did kill him?" she asked, her words gushing out.

Jillian's eyes widened. "Don't even think like that. Your brother will investigate whether you've had any contact with the deceased. If you haven't, we'll go with the argument that you were framed. The real killer will have left a clue somewhere, and our brothers will find out who he is."

Another glimmer of hope surfaced, and Blair stood and hugged her friend. "Thank you."

Jillian nodded and then left. Once alone, the black veil of uncertainty descended. Perhaps the real question she needed to ask herself was whether she was capable of such a crime. Someone had grabbed her—that much was clear—but had there been a struggle? Would she have been strong enough to wrestle the gun from his hand and shoot him?

She dropped back down onto the chair and buried her head in her arms. *If anyone up there is listening, please help me.*

Chapter Three

WORRYING ABOUT BLAIR had kept Ronan from sleeping last night. As much as he wanted to see her, to tell her he would do everything in his power to find the killer, for her sake, he'd sit tight.

Ronan downed the rest of his strong morning coffee, locked up the guesthouse that belonged to Connor's parents, and headed out. As soon as he had a moment, he'd look for a place of his own. As much as he appreciated the free accommodations, he was here to stay now that he'd found his mate. He didn't want to take advantage of their hospitality.

As he drove into work, Ronan avoided taking the road by the sheriff's department since he'd be too tempted to stop and see Blair. If he did talk to her, he'd want to let her know she wasn't alone and then blurt out they were mates by mistake. Given her state of mind, most likely it wouldn't go over well.

Ronan could still recall that first moment when they'd locked eyes. It was as if a thirty-five year old engine that had been sitting idle its whole life had finally been plugged in. Sparks flew and the much-needed oil had breathed life into the machine. His body's reaction was similar. Blair's had not been. His bones had cracked, and his teeth had sharpened, but he didn't get the sense that Blair had a clue they were fated to be together. He found it incredibly strange and quite unnerving that she didn't. Wasn't every shifter supposed to know who they were destined to be with?

His father had told him several stories about shifters, but too many of the tales contradicted each other, so maybe he'd been misinformed. Discussing sex with his fellow shifters wasn't something he even considered since his Clan in Vermont hadn't been the sharing type.

Ronan was, and probably always would be, a loner. It was safer that way. His sister claimed the fact he'd accepted the job at McKinnon and Associates meant he was changing, but he wasn't so sure. He took the job partly because Lexi was the only family he had left, and he wanted to take advantage of the fact she now lived in Silver Lake.

Before he could solve that age-old problem of mating and each party's differing reactions, he arrived at the office. Now that Timothy Delahart was no longer alive, Ronan's reason for coming to Silver Lake no longer existed.

As he walked past Connor's open office door, his boss motioned him in. Kalan was inside, and a sledgehammer went to town inside his chest. His visit most likely had to do with Blair.

"Kalan," Ronan said, trying to keep the panic from his voice. They shook hands.

"I'm glad you're here," Kalan said. "Have a seat. Connor and I have something to discuss with you."

"What is it?"

"Judge Hollars is out of town, so I couldn't see him in person to ask about bail. I did however contact the district attorney who is a—"

"Kalan," Connor demanded. "Get to the point."

"Sure. The district attorney contacted the judge for me. Hollars is letting Blair out on bail under one circumstance. She must be supervised. For some reason, the judge seems to think she's a flight risk. The man's a dick, but at least he agreed to bail."

"We'd like you and Jackson to watch over her," Connor added.

Ronan's heart sprinted. As much as he wanted to be near her, it would be pure torture to be so close and not touch her. "Why me?"

"You don't have any cases right now," Connor shot back.

That was true. He mentally clicked through the schedules of the other team members, and they each had one or two cases they were investigating. "When is she being released?"

"The order came in an hour ago. She needs someone to pick her up," Connor said. "How about bringing her here?"

"Why here?" His mind wasn't operating on all cylinders. His wolf was too busy rejoicing.

"Since I'm convinced Blair is innocent, I'm going to assume the worst happened to her—that she witnessed something she shouldn't have, and the real killer wants to make sure she doesn't say anything."

His protective instincts shot into high gear. "Got it. I'll make sure she remains safe. I'll pick up a few things from the guesthouse so I can stay here at night. I'll sleep on the sofa in my office."

"You don't have to do that," Connor said. "No one can breach our security. Even if they did, he'd never find the switch that opens the panel to the safe room."

"I'd feel better if Blair had someone to talk to if she has a nightmare." Ronan probably should have come up with a different reason, but that was the truth.

"Suit yourself. Jackson will be keeping an eye on her too, but with you around, he can spend more time with his mate. If you need to do something, Jackson can take over the protection detail."

Ronan pushed back his chair. "I'll head out now."

Kalan stood. "I'll follow you. I need to make sure there isn't a glitch with the paperwork."

They both left by the front door. All during the drive, Ronan battled with his inner animal. Because Blair didn't know him very well, and might not be comfortable around him, he'd have to act totally professional. One hint that he wanted her and she might complain to her brother—an event he wanted to avoid at all costs. The poor woman had enough to deal with besides a horny mate.

That's not true, his wolf shot back. *She'll need to be comforted after her ordeal. She'll need a shoulder to cry on.*

She's strong. Blair won't appreciate anyone feeling sorry for.

You're just saying that so you can keep your distance. You're a chicken shit.

Ronan highly disliked it when his wolf argued with him—especially when he was right. Ronan couldn't blame his wolf for his antsy attitude. Ronan had denied his baser needs for far too long.

Kalan waited for him while he parked. Ronan rushed up the department steps where Kalan led him inside. "Stay here while I check to see if all the paperwork is in order. Then I'll escort Blair out."

"Sure." Ronan paced the large entranceway, trying to calm his libido. Twice, he'd had to hide his arms behind his back because fur had sprouted on his hands. Only a few of the employees were shifters, and exhibiting any signs of being a werewolf would be disastrous.

Ronan needed to get a grip. Ever since he'd found Blair, he'd had no more control than a randy teenager. Hell, he stalked killers and thugs for a living. One woman shouldn't throw him for a loop—but she did.

A few minutes later, voices sounded. It was her voice—sweet yet strong. Even before Blair came into view, his body turned traitor.

Down boy, he told his randy wolf. *Remember, no woman has ever wanted our lifestyle.*

It was why he'd kept to himself all these years. Lexi said his unkempt beard was his way of pushing women away. He wanted to believe it was his way of waiting for his mate to walk into his life.

"Ronan is going to make sure you stay safe," Kalan told his sister as he escorted her near—close enough for her delicate scent to seep into his pores—a scent that translated to beautiful colors of pinks and purples. He closed his eyes for a moment in an attempt to block out her scent, but he failed the moment he opened them again.

Blair looked over at him and pressed her lips together. That wasn't the reaction he was looking for. Damn. There hadn't even been a flicker of joy or lust or recognition that they belonged together. No doubt these next few weeks were going to be worse than swimming unarmed in a sea full of sharks.

WHILE BLAIR WAS relieved the judge had granted her bail, the idea of being kept in a room in the basement of her brother's workplace didn't sit well with her at all. The one consolation was that she'd been given permission to go to work. She would cherish the hours of being surrounded by her friends and patients.

Ronan was staring at her, looking fierce though a bit uncomfortable. *Say something.* "I'm sorry you got the short straw and have to play bodyguard."

His eyes lit up for a moment before the flame extinguished. "I'm happy to do it."

He looked about as happy as a wolf caught in a steel trap. He shouldn't complain though. Life imprisonment wasn't looming over his head.

Kalan placed a hand on her shoulder. "Do whatever Ronan says. Remember, it's possible you might be the next target."

She squinted at him. The oaf didn't have to remind her. "I still think that if I'd seen a murder—like you've suggested—I would be dead already. Why would someone leave a witness?"

"Good question. Remind me to ask him when I find him."

Blair didn't need to be arguing with Kalan. "Don't worry about me. I'll be good, I promise." She stood on her toes and kissed his cheek. "Thank you for everything."

"Just stay safe. It'll all work out." Kalan squeezed her shoulder and then returned to work.

This was it. Time to find out if a maniac was out there ready to pounce. Blair faced Ronan. He was watching her with such intensity, she almost felt as if he was undressing her. She shoved that stab of lust aside and inhaled. "I'm ready."

As soon as they reached the door, Ronan held up his hand. "Let me check to see that it's clear."

"Aren't you overreacting a little?" *Please say yes.* "No one is going to make a move in front of the sheriff's department."

One brow rose. It was almost as if he was debating whether to lecture her on the dos and don'ts of being a bodyguard. "We can't be too sure. Remember, someone killed Delahart in broad daylight." He scanned the area. "The killer might not exactly be the sharpest tool."

"Maybe it wasn't premeditated. The body was found near the exit door—or so Kalan said. Who does that, especially around quitting time next to a business?"

"You have an excellent point," Ronan said, not making eye contact. "Okay, it looks good. Stay close."

Blair didn't know why she was thrilled by his small praise. It shouldn't matter. Ronan Laramie was her bodyguard and nothing more. If only her bear hadn't decided to go into hibernation after her last fiasco, Blair might be given some guidance.

Being a man of few words was a good thing. It was a lot better than being protected by someone who would pummel her with questions.

Sure, Ronan was hotter than sin, but she'd fallen for the wrong type of man in the past, and she wouldn't do that again. Lesson learned. Her bear had warned her that Jared Henderson was not her mate, but she was too damn stubborn to listen.

I'm sorry. Please wake up, she begged her inner bear. *Jared was really convincing.*

As usual, her bear didn't answer. It didn't matter. Blair didn't want to think about Jared Henderson. Right now, she needed to focus on proving her innocence, not on enjoying a tangled, sensual journey with Ronan, a man she barely knew.

She had thought Jackson, her other brother, would have been assigned to watch her, but Kalan said he was working on another case and that he would step in for Ronan if need be.

With Ronan's gaze still on the streets instead of on her, he opened the door to his Jeep and motioned she slide in.

Once he closed the door, he dashed over to his side. "Put your seatbelt on," he said.

Dang, Blair never forgot. She must have lost more than her memory. "Would you mind if I stop at my house first?" she asked. "I need to pick up a few things."

After checking the side view mirrors, Ronan started the engine and pulled onto the road. He didn't speak for a full minute. "Sure. Where do you live?"

When she gave him directions, she didn't miss the tic around his mouth. Clearly, he disapproved of her living so far away from the family unit. Too freaking bad. She had her reasons. Good ones too. At least she'd moved back to town, though if her one and only job offer hadn't been in Silver Lake, she would have gone elsewhere.

"Do you mind if I swing by my place first?" Ronan asked. "It's on the way, and I need to grab some stuff too. Then I can drive you to your house."

She inwardly groaned at coming so close to her parents' place. "You're taking this job seriously, aren't you? You don't need to babysit me. I promise I won't run away. My parents had to put up their entire estate for bail."

Ronan glanced over at her. "It's not you fleeing town that I'm worried about. It's the killer coming after you that we need to be concerned with."

Shivers crawled up her spine. "You sound like Kalan. What clues do you have that there is a killer gunning for me?"

"Nothing concrete, but if you didn't kill Timothy Delahart, someone else did. The blood on your shirt implies you were close— close enough for the shooter to have seen you. And the GSR implies you fired a gun at something or someone."

"I know." She looked out the window and watched as he drove down all the familiar roads. She needed to stop by to thank her parents for their support, but she wasn't ready yet for that uncomfortable conversation. Blair would call them from the safe room and figure out a good time to visit. "I'm convinced someone must have put a curse on me. It's the only explanation. With my memory all but erased, the killer has nothing to fear." Ronan was a Wendayan and wouldn't think that concept to be too far fetched.

"That's logical except for the fact that curses or spells have been known to wear off."

"If he was smart, he would make it last forever."

Ronan glanced over at her, and she caught the briefest of smiles. "The operative word being smart, which most likely he is not. You already stated why. Killing in an alley in broad daylight implies it was spontaneous. Besides, I doubt even the most powerful witch can make spells last forever."

"You have a point. The dark witch from Cargonia who put the spell on Zane Barons had claimed it would last forever, and that didn't happen. When his mate came near, he awoke from his forever sleep."

"See?"

Blair turned her thoughts back to the killing. "What do you think went down in the alley?"

Ronan bounced his focus between his mirrors and the road. "We might never know, but I've been chasing after Delahart for months. I'm guessing there was some kind of altercation. Knowing him, it was probably a double-cross. Killing Delahart might not have been the plan."

"That might explain the murder in broad daylight."

Ronan approached her parents' place and slowed. "Do you want to stop by your folks while I grab a few things? I'm sure they'd like to see that you're okay. I'll only be a few minutes."

She didn't want to, but she couldn't think of a good excuse to tell him why not. Blair certainly didn't need Ronan telling her brother that she didn't want to speak with their parents after her humiliating arrest. "That would be great, thanks."

Blair pointed out which house was theirs. Her mom's car sat in the drive, and her dad's was most likely in the garage. There was no turning back now.

Ronan stopped the car. "Once I see you go inside, I'll pick up my stuff and then come back. I'll be waiting outside whenever you're ready."

She was about to tell him he didn't have to sit outside, that he could come in, but then she decided she wasn't ready for her mom to pummel him with questions. Blair never brought anyone home, and she could only imagine what it would imply if she did. It didn't matter than Connor had assigned Ronan to watch her. "Thanks."

When she reached the front door, she rang the bell then depressed the handle. It was unlocked. Her parents never seemed to fear anyone.

"Hello?" she called as soon as she stepped into the foyer. The house smelled of fresh baked bread, and her stomach grumbled. Then fond memories of growing up here reached out and embraced her, erasing some of her doubts.

Feet scurried, and a moment later, both her mother and father rushed into the foyer. Her mom was wearing an apron, her forehead was damp, and she looked as if she'd slaved over a hot stove for way too long.

"Blair," her mother cried as she hugged her tight. Her plump figure enveloped her in love, helping to soothe the recent aches. "Oh, sweetheart, how are you holding up? Kalan briefly told me what happened. It's so terrible."

"I'm okay, Mom."

When her mother let go, her father leaned in and kissed her cheek. "We've been so worried. We wanted to see you, but Kalan asked that we stay away. He said that our visit might make it harder for you."

"It probably was better that you didn't see me in that dark and dingy place. As it is, I really need to shower."

"I can only imagine. Come into the living room and tell us everything. You know your brother; he is so closed mouthed." Her mom brushed a slightly graying wisp of hair from her face.

She had to be talking about Kalan. Jackson never shut up. "It's his job not to say anything."

"We know, dear. Can I get you something to drink?" her mom asked.

"Iced tea?" Funny, when she had been in that dark room, all she could think about was her mom's sun tea. "By any chance, do you have any banana bread?" Her mom baked some every Sunday.

"I sure do. Sit and chat with your dad while I bring it right out."

Once her mom left, Blair turned to her father. "I don't know what Kalan told you, but it couldn't be much since I can't remember anything."

"Take a seat and start from the beginning." Her father slipped off his reading glasses and shoved them into his top pocket as he plopped down on his favorite recliner.

Blair told him about leaving work at the usual hour. "All I remember is returning home, but I don't remember anything in between the time I left work and when I arrived at my house. The strangest part is that I was totally unaware that I'd missed a chunk of time."

Her mother came in bearing a tall glass of iced tea topped with a wedge of lemon and a sprig of mint, along with a plate of banana bread. The scent was heavenly.

"Thanks. I was just telling Dad—"

"I heard."

Of course she did. Good ole shifter hearing. "Anyway, when I saw that my shirt was covered in blood, I panicked. After I made sure I wasn't injured, I called Kalan. It was only when he found out a man had been murdered in the alley behind work that he took me in for questioning. Turns out the blood belonged to the dead man."

"There has to be an explanation," her mom said as she sat on the sofa next to Blair. "I bet you saw him and tried to help."

"That's what I thought. It might be true, but it doesn't explain everything."

"What do you mean?" her dad asked.

Here came the hard part. "They tested my hands for gunshot residue and found some. Apparently, I shot the gun. Whether it was the one that killed the man, we don't know."

Indignation raced across her face. "Someone has framed you," her mother said so matter-of-factly that Blair wanted to smile. She loved that they had total faith in her. Too bad, it wasn't always warranted.

"I'd like to believe that," Blair said.

Her father leaned forward, his forehead furrowed. "How do you explain the memory loss?"

"That's the big question. I can't. The only explanation is that I walked out of the back door and stumbled onto a shooting. Either I was traumatized to the point of forgetting, or someone did something to me."

"Hmm, that could be. A weapon in an enclosed space such as an alley makes a lot of noise. I would have thought someone would have rushed out to find out what was going on." Her father almost sounded as if he doubted her story.

"Not that anyone has told me. Maybe he used a silencer. I'm sure Kalan will ask everyone who was at work that day if they heard anything, but it can get rather loud in the office, and the side door is pretty far from the street," Blair said.

"If someone put a spell on you, it would have taken time. It's not like the witch can just wave a hand."

"I couldn't say."

Her dad looked off to the side. "It seems strange that none of your coworkers left by the same back door."

"Not many park in back. I wish I had answers," she said. Blair took a large bite of the delicious bread and then chugged half her tea. She didn't remember anything tasting better. "I hate to run, but my bodyguard is waiting outside for me."

Her dad wagged a finger at her and smiled, though the joy didn't reach his eyes. "Okay, but just make sure you don't skip town. We had to mortgage the whole house to post bail."

Horror swallowed her whole again. "I never would. I promise."

"I know, hon," he said as he rubbed his chest, acting as if his heartburn was flaring up again. "Kalan mentioned you needing a bodyguard. Something about the real killer might try to come after you since you witnessed the crime."

Here she thought Kalan was close mouthed about what happened. "Yes, but I doubt the killer will do anything unless I start remembering."

"Maybe it's better if you don't," her mom said, patting Blair's hand.

"There are times when I have to agree with you, but the need to know runs strong. If they find evidence that proves someone else killed that Delahart man I'm good not learning the details. But what if I have to go to trial? I might be convicted if I don't remember."

"Don't think like that."

Blair stood and her parents followed. She didn't need to worry them more than she already had. "I promise to leave the investigation to Kalan and Dalton. If Jackson wants to help, I'd welcome it, too."

"So who is watching over you?" her dad asked.

"Connor assigned Ronan Laramie, but if he needs to do something, Jackson will help out."

Her father nodded. "Ronan is a fine young man. You said he's waiting outside?"

"He should be back by now. He had to stop over at the McKinnon guesthouse where he's staying to pick up some things."

"Why don't you ask him in?" his dad asked.

That was the last thing she wanted or needed. "There isn't time. Connor told him to take me directly to the safe room, but since Ronan dropped me off here before he stopped to pick up a few things, we're already running late. If we don't show up there soon, Connor will think something has happened." She finished the rest of her iced tea and chowed down the banana bread. "This is amazing, Mom. I didn't realize how hungry I was."

"I imagine they didn't feed you a five-star meal over there."

"That's an understatement, though even if they had, I'm not sure I could have eaten much."

She had the most wonderful parents in the world. It was why she hated to disappoint them.

Tell them what happened in Georgia. They'll understand.

As much as she wanted to, it had been three years. They had enough to deal with. "I'm sorry to put you through all this."

"Don't worry about us, darling," her mom said. "We'll get through it."

After a round of hugs and kisses, Blair left to begin her weeks of solitude.

Chapter Four

"BLAIR, I WAS so worried about you," Ainsley said over the phone. "Jackson told me what happened."

During her darkest hours in that cell, Blair had thought about sending some kind of message to Ainsley and asking her to visit. With her friend's ability to become invisible, she could have shown up with no one the wiser. However, Blair didn't need her friend to get into trouble. And if Ainsley remained invisible, Blair didn't know if they could talk to each other.

Stretching out on the safe room's bed, Blair let the comfort of being secure seep into her. "It's still a nightmare. What if I really did kill him?"

"I've known you forever. You aren't capable of killing anyone."

She hoped that was true. "Let's hope the jury believes that."

"They'll find the killer long before you go to trial."

The thought of being incarcerated erased the bubble of safety she'd just experienced. They chatted a bit about the possible causes for her memory loss and what everyone was doing to help. "All I can do is wait and see," Blair said. "I trust Kalan, Dalton, and Jackson to figure everything out."

"I agree. Other than being stuck in that room at night, how's it going with Ronan?"

Hearing his name sent her thoughts in the absolute wrong direction. "He's fine."

Ainsley chuckled. "Fine? Come on. If I weren't mated to your brother, I'd take a second look."

"I need to concentrate on staying out of the killer's crosshairs, not think about some make out session."

"Make out session? I'm talking about hot sex to take your mind off your troubles."

"Pu-lease." She didn't have time for this—or rather she didn't want to discuss it.

"Blair, I'm serious. You haven't looked at a man since that incident with Jared."

"It was hardly an incident as you put it. And I don't want to discuss it. I made a huge mistake thinking he was my mate. You met Jared; he could act really charming." As well as deceitful, along with a host of other unscrupulous names.

Ainsley didn't respond at first, but Blair could almost sense her mind searching the database brain of hers. "I know, but what about Ronan? Could he be the one?"

What was she talking about? "No! At least I don't think so. Hell, I can't trust my instincts anymore. My bear might—never mind."

"What were you going to say?" Ainsley liked to prod.

"Nothing, okay?" Blair hadn't meant to sound so agitated, but she'd had a bad day.

"Fine, but I'm just saying, I think Ronan is a fine catch."

"Whether he is or isn't shouldn't matter. He's here to keep me safe. That's all. Now can we talk about something else?"

Ainsley chuckled. "Sure. Do you have any idea when you'll be coming back to work?"

"I plan to return on Monday."

"Really? Are you sure? I mean that man was murdered in our back alley. Won't it give you the creeps being at work?"

"Why should it? I have no memory of the incident," Blair said.

"That's true."

Like they always did, they wandered into familiar territory, talking about the clients they both treated. Often, Ainsley would treat someone first, plying her acupuncturist skills, and then they'd follow up with physical therapy with Blair.

A knock sounded on her outer door and she jumped. "Oh. Someone's here. I gotta go."

"It must be Ronan. Jackson just walked in, so it can't be him."

"I'll let you go. Love you."

"Love you back," Ainsley said.

Blair shoved off from the bed, rushed across the room, and then slid back the deadbolt. When she pulled open the door, her body sizzled with desire. Oh my. *Do you think he's the one?* she asked her bear.

As usual, her bear didn't respond. *Wake up, damn it,* she said. *I need you to help me.*

More silence. Her bear had been dormant for three years. She didn't know why she'd hoped her animal would wake up now.

I told you I'm sorry. I messed up. Okay? I need you now.

Finally, Blair stopped asking and studied Ronan. His eyes were black with intermittent swirls of amber, and his shoulders were ramrod straight. She had the sense he was working hard to stay in control. Only why?

"Hey, Ronan, is something wrong?"

"No. I just wanted to make sure you're okay."

"Why wouldn't I be? No one can get to me here." She didn't understand why he had come all the way downstairs. Was it to say goodnight? At that thought, her impression of him changed. Perhaps he wasn't the hard ass he tried to portray.

"I thought I heard you talking to someone."

Shifters had good hearing, but no one could hear from upstairs, unless he had been standing outside her door. While she didn't like eavesdroppers, it was his job to check up on her. "I was speaking with Ainsley. She and I used to room together in school, and we work at the same place now."

Ronan cleared his throat. "Good to know. I wanted to tell you that when you wake tomorrow morning, I might be gone."

An unexpected tightening of her stomach took her off guard.

The rest of the team would be upstairs, including her brother, so she'd be perfectly safe. Not knowing where Ronan would be disturbed her for some reason. "Where are you going?"

"Not that I don't think your brother isn't capable of finding the culprit, but I do have some extra useful senses that others don't possess. I want to do a little snooping on my own."

"Oh." She was at a loss for words.

"If you need anything, just ask Jackson or any of the men."

"I will."

Ronan broke eye contact and strode off. There was something odd about his visit, but she couldn't quite figure it out. One minute he was this total professional and the next his eyes were swirls of amber and brown. If so much of his face wasn't already covered in a scruffy beard, she might have noticed some other evidence of shifter behavior. Interesting. *Does that mean he likes me?*

Stop it. She couldn't think about mates or sex or even dating. She needed this murder charge to go away first.

AS SOON AS Ronan reached the office upstairs, he plastered his back against the wall. He never should have told Blair he'd heard her talking. While she didn't ask how he'd been able to hear her, he didn't miss the slight change in her scent—one from happy to a bit more agitated. He'd been a fool, but it had been his wolf who'd wanted to know if she felt the intense pull that was driving them crazy. From the occasional laughter, she was speaking with a close friend, and friends like that shared everything.

Don't blame me, buddy. You wanted to know too, his wolf responded.

What's done is done.

Unfortunately, he'd arrived too late in the conversation to hear anything about Blair's feelings for him. But that was probably for the best. Right now, he needed to push back this whole mate thing until after he helped prove her innocence.

Tomorrow, he planned to check out the crime scene and sniff around. While two days had passed since the murder, there might be a lingering scent that could lead him to the real killer. Colors had a way of staying around long after the person was gone.

He planned to snap some photos and take a video of the area. Even though Blair walked down that back alley every day, a picture might help jar her memory. Even a slightly different angle could provide the senses with a new perspective.

If that failed to jar her memory, he might ask Sam Pompley if he could see into her mind and help her retrieve what she'd lost. Normally, Lexi's mate inserted false images into a person's mind to convince him what he saw was different from reality, but he might be able to read minds, too.

Tomorrow, he'd investigate and hopefully find some answers.

AS SOON AS Ronan neared the alleyway behind Blair's work, he was met by one of the sheriff department's deputies.

"Sorry, sir, but this is a crime scene. I can't let anyone near."

"Who's the lead on the case?" Ronan asked. While he knew the answer, he wanted to make sure the officer was aware of it.

"Detective Dalton Garner."

Kalan Murdoch's partner. It made sense they wouldn't want Kalan to be in charge. After all, his sister was a suspect. Ronan pulled out his phone and called Kalan. While he waited for him to answer, Ronan strolled out of the deputy's earshot.

"Murdoch." Squeaky roller chairs, along with a few shouts echoed in the background. He must be at the station.

"Kalan, this is Ronan."

"Is Blair okay?" His words were strung tighter than a guy wire.

He should have included that in the greeting. "She's fine. Jackson and Connor are keeping her company. Listen, I'd like to snoop around the crime scene, but one of your deputies is keeping a tight lid on the situation."

"Gonzalez is new. It's his job."

"Do you think I could take a look around? I won't touch anything."

"What do you hope to find?"

"I thought I'd take some photos in the hopes it can jar Blair's memory. I know she cuts through the alley every day, but there might be something that will trigger an image. I also want to sniff around to see if I recognize any of the scents."

"It's worth a try. I'll have Dalton call Gonzalez and tell him you have clearance."

"Thanks."

Ronan didn't have to wait long before Dalton called. Gonzalez looked up and motioned him under the police tape.

As Ronan drew closer to the scene, his senses kicked in, and some familiar odor caused him to falter. He blinked away the quick wash of color entering his mind. The winds must be playing tricks on him, or else it was Blair's scent that was still in his head, diluting the reality.

Focus! Without further thought, he moved over to where the man, or rather the werewolf, had bled out. While the body was now in the morgue, a dark red area stained the dirt. Delahart's scent was overpowering, masking most of the other odors. Damn.

The only way he could identify whose scent belonged to who was by its colors. Most people catalogued odors by referencing it to something they could identify. They might say it smelled like popcorn or rotten eggs. Ronan wasn't built like that. He saw colors as scents—millions of them—and each one represented a distinct person—just like a fingerprint.

But similar to fingerprints, he needed a reference point. And like a bloodhound, he could follow a color until the kaleidoscope of images broke up and dissipated. Then the trail would grow cold. When he met someone, he'd know right away if he'd met that person before. A scent never lied.

Needless to say, Ronan was a dangerous man to any criminal.

Thankfully, only a handful of people were aware of his talent, and he intended to keep it that way.

Determined to help Blair, he inhaled to identify who else had been there recently. Kalan's and Dalton's identifying markers were fairly strong, which made sense since they probably had been in this area today or late last night. Kalan's scent was blue with swirls of green and orange mixed in, while Dalton's was almost yellowish-white with streaks of brown interspersed at random intervals. Then there was Blair's fragrance. He inhaled again to revel in her delicious scent. Hers was a delicate purple with light pink highlights, dotted with wisps of green.

But there were more colors in the air, fainter yet distinct. One was midnight blue accented by deep maroon, yet Ronan couldn't identify that person. The question was whether it belonged to the killer. It wasn't Gonzalez's. That one he'd already eliminated.

With the scents now locked into his brain, he continued to study the surroundings. The murder occurred about six feet from the door leading out of Blair's workplace. She would have seen and heard two men arguing within seconds of leaving work. If she'd spotted a weapon, he couldn't imagine what had gone through her mind. Assuming she'd identified the danger, why not sneak back inside or at least scream for help?

To eliminate the reason why she hadn't escaped, he slipped on a glove and tugged on the door. Locked. That explained why Blair hadn't run back in.

"You can only exit. Door automatically locks," Gonzalez called.

Ronan waved. "Thanks."

He wanted Blair to remember, but maybe regaining her memory wouldn't be for the best. Being able to identify the killer could lead to an arrest, but it could also cause the killer to come after her, before the cops could catch him.

Frustration bit Ronan in the butt. As much as he wanted to spend more time at the crime scene, he didn't want to contaminate it. He'd return after the cops had finished processing everything.

After taking a few photos from different angles, along with a video, he headed back to the office. As much as he didn't want to put Blair through more questions, he hoped something would help unlock the mystery. But before he approached her, he wanted to see what Sam could tell him about putting memories into a person's head. Was he aware of a person who could remove them? That would be a key to solving this case.

Chapter Five

WHEN RONAN ENTERED the building, Blair's purple and pink scent swirled around, doing a dance around his body and then seeping into every pore. That wasn't good. He had a killer to find before he indulged in his fantasies with her.

Can't you block out her fragrance for a little while? he begged his wolf. *I have work to do.*

I haven't seen such rich colors in a long time. Her scent is intoxicating, his wolf shot back.

If you want Blair to remain alive, then stand down. I have to be able to focus.

Ronan's wolf huffed and growled, but he thankfully stopped whining.

When Ronan passed through the main room, Blair wasn't there, for which he was thankful. He needed to see Sam first.

Ronan found him in his office. "Got a minute?" Ronan asked.

"Sure."

He explained his need to have Blair's memories returned. "You told me that you can insert false memories into a person's mind, but is there any way you can look into Blair's mind and see what she can't recall?" Ronan asked. He pulled up a chair and sat.

"I wish I could," Sam said. "Sometimes I can read a person's mind, but he or she needs to be actively thinking about a specific thing."

That wouldn't help. "It was worth a shot." He studied his friend and then asked Sam, "Do you know of anyone who can erase memories completely?"

"Hell no! Anyone who can do that would have to be powerful—almost godlike. I can only replace a memory with another one."

His protective side flared. Battling a demon would be suicidal, though he had heard one of the Wendayans—Missy Berta—had managed to take one down. "Maybe we should contact Vinea to see if she's aware of any gods from the dark realm who are here. I'd hate to think there's a conspiracy going on that we're not aware of."

Sam's features tightened. While Connor claimed Sam had forgiven the goddess for almost stealing his powers, Ronan wasn't convinced Vinea would ever be his favorite person despite having been cleansed. On the other hand, his reaction could be a result of imagining what damage a demon could do.

"I think it's a good idea, but why not ask Ophelia? Rumor has it she's always in the know."

"Ophelia?" He had a lot of people he still needed to meet.

Sam explained that she was the town's most powerful witch. "If someone put a spell on Blair, Ophelia might be able to undo it."

Excitement sprinted through him. "How do I contact her?"

"Ask Rye to ask his mate. Izzy seems to have a connection to her."

That sounded like a plan. "Thanks."

Before he went the witch route, Ronan wanted to see Blair. Following her scent, he located her in Jackson's office.

Ronan tapped on the slightly open door then entered. Blair was sitting in a chair reading. When she looked up, hope filled her eyes. Her beautiful light auburn hair was pulled back into a ponytail, making her appear even younger. Now he'd have to disappoint her. "Hey, can we talk?" he asked.

"Sure."

"Let's let Jackson get back to work. How about coming into my office?" He didn't need her brother seeing any physical changes occur when Ronan spent too much time around Blair.

She stood and then followed him down the hallway. "What did you find out?"

Though her words came out sounding calm, her scent was shooting waves of different shades of gray—all indicating fear.

Ronan opened his door and motioned she step inside. Not wanting her to feel like this was an inquisition, he dragged over two chairs and placed them opposite each other, close enough to indicate this would be a friendly exchange. "I want you to take a look at some pictures."

"Pictures?" Her eyes opened wide.

"They're not of anything bad. I stood with my back to the workplace door where you exited and shot a short video."

"Why?" Her defensive tone gave him pause. She might not be ready for this.

Ronan huffed out a sigh. "I was hoping you might see something that would help you remember."

"I told you, it's still a blank."

He held up a hand. "Okay, but humor me, please?" He loaded up the short video on his phone and handed it to her. "I know you walk this alley every day, but try to imagine being there now."

She took the phone and watched the video. Her gaze searched the screen. Clearly, she was trying, but the reddish aura implied accelerated tension. "Nope."

Clearly, she was telling the truth. "Thanks for taking a look. Sam suggested seeing a woman by the name of Ophelia to see if she can reverse the spell."

Blair nodded. "My lawyer suggested the same thing."

He waited for her to add something, but when she didn't he continued. "Do you want me to set it up?"

Ronan thought Blair would jump at the chance, but she glanced away. Her gray scent turned darker as her mouth twisted. When she sucked in her bottom lip, his wolf—who had more or less been good for a while—shot a shit ton of lust through his veins, and Ronan's cock instantly hardened, forcing him to cross his ankle over his knee to block the view.

"I guess so, but what if I remember something and the killer finds out? He'll come after me."

Honesty ran in his blood. "That is why either Jackson or I need to be with you at all times."

"Even when I go to work?"

Ronan didn't relish that part of the job, as he was a hunter by nature, but he wouldn't leave Blair vulnerable. "Yes. Remember, the judge insisted."

"Fine. Let's see if Ophelia can help."

Ronan pulled out his phone. His sister had already loaded it with every number he might ever need. McKinnon and Associates was lucky to have her. While he rarely had the need to contact the Alpha of the Clan, this was important.

To his delight, Rye answered on the first ring, and Ronan explained that Blair would like to contact Ophelia.

"I'll ask Izzy and then get back with you once something has been set up." He then gave Ronan a few warnings about what to expect, such as the fact she wasn't the easiest person to get answers out of.

"I appreciate the chance to meet with her. We're at our wit's end."

"I understand."

Ronan disconnected and smiled, not because he was happy, but because he wanted to assure Blair that she wasn't alone in this journey. "Now, we wait."

"HAVE YOU EVER met this witch before?" Ronan asked as he pulled in front of Izzy's former home.

"When I was like ten. I remember being so scared the first time." Blair looked off, but instead of seeing the gray shimmer of fear, it had a wash of yellow, implying her memory was now a good one.

"Why were you scared?" he asked.

"I thought she might turn me into a frog or something."

Ronan chuckled, enjoying hearing about her youth. "I take it she did no such thing?"

"No. Ophelia was very sweet, but I swear she looked hundreds of years old back then, which was why she frightened me."

When he was a kid, he thought anyone over fifty was ancient. "Why would a ten-year old have need of a witch's advice?"

She smiled and his insides lit up. "I really wanted to have some Wendayan powers like a few of my friends—Izzy mostly—so Mom let me ask Ophelia for some. Even though my mother tried to explain that I needed to be born a Wendayan in order to possess magic, I wasn't convinced."

"You can have those powers if you mate with a Wendayan," he added. *Like me.*

"That is true," she said but her color changed once more and was now tinged with red. Some memory must have disturbed her, but now wasn't the time to delve into it.

"Did Ophelia let you down easily?" Ronan asked.

"Yes. She listened to my reasons and then said she'd try real hard to give me some powers, but that she couldn't promise anything."

Ronan pushed open his Jeep's door. "I'm glad she wasn't mean."

"Me too. I actually left that afternoon feeling that if I wished hard enough, I could create some magic."

She certainly was creating magic inside his body. "I'm glad she didn't dash a young girl's dreams."

Before he had the chance to help her out, Blair had exited. The men in her life must not have been gentlemen.

As he scoped out the area for the witch, as well as any other unwanted visitors, Blair brushed his arm and pointed. All it took was that one contact for his brain to fuzz and his damn wolf to howl. After a quick check with his tongue that his teeth hadn't poked out, he exhaled.

This is important, so behave, he told his wolf.

But she smells so fucking good.

Like I don't know that? Ronan believed he had it worse than any shifter in the world because of his acute sense of smell. Blair distracted him like no one ever had.

A woman in a long gray dress stepped from behind a tree. Blair grabbed his hand for a second and squeezed. "There she is. Just like I remember her."

Her brief touch made his balls ache. Most likely, his eyes were growing more amber by the minute. Forcing himself to study the older woman, his cock thankfully deflated. "Do you want to speak with her alone?" he asked, hoping she'd say no.

"No. Come with me. Izzy claims the witch talks in circles, and I might forget everything she tells me." The brief smile that followed caused his wolf to clamor for release.

Stupid wolf. "Let's go."

PRICKS OF EXCITEMENT blended with stabs of uncertainty. Blair wanted Ophelia to help her, but at the same time, she wasn't sure she wanted to remember that tragic event. But if Blair never learned the truth, it might slowly drive her crazy.

"Blair! You've grown up to be such a lovely woman." Ophelia held out her hands, and Blair grasped them. Her gnarled warmth sank into her.

For a brief moment, Blair thought Ophelia might tell her that while her bear was in hibernation, she'd awaken soon. Apparently, that wasn't the case.

"Thank you." Ophelia let go and her gaze swung over to Ronan. When her eyes and face softened and a broader smile appeared, Blair tensed. Why? Surely it wasn't jealousy! "This is Ronan Laramie. He's my bodyguard."

"Bodyguard, you say. Interesting." Her smile remained.

What was she implying? Everything Ophelia said had a hidden meaning. Blair was about to explain that he was a bit more than that, but she didn't want to get his hopes up. Yes, Ronan was sexy and the type of man she wanted, but she didn't trust herself not to make the same mistake twice.

"Ronan Laramie. You're Lexi's brother, right?"

Now how did she know that? Duh, because Ophelia knows everything.

Ronan didn't even blink. "Yes, ma'am."

Ophelia returned her gaze to Blair. "What can I help you with today? Izzy only briefly told me what happened. I'm sorry you were caught up in such nastiness."

A murder was more than just nastiness. "I can't remember anything about the event. It's like someone erased my memory."

All cheer in her face evaporated. "Even after a few days, nothing's come back?"

"No." Worry dug a big hole in her stomach.

"It doesn't sound like a spell then—more like a curse."

Ronan pressed closer, but it barely helped quell the tremors in her hands.

"So you can't reverse it?" he asked.

"Young man, I have my limits. Now, stand aside and let me see what I can do." Ophelia faced her again and held out her hands once more. Blair clasped them. When Ophelia closed her eyes, so did Blair.

The old witch hummed, and her grip tightened. When Ophelia's tone changed, Blair's heart wiggled and then fluttered. Ophelia let go, and Blair opened her eyes. "Well?" she asked.

"A darkness is near."

"A darkness? What does that mean? What should I do?"

"That's all I can say." Ophelia twisted toward Ronan and added, "Protect her the best that you can."

"I will."

Ophelia turned and seemed to float toward the woods. Izzy had mentioned that once the session was over, it was best to leave, but Blair had so many more questions to ask. Only when Ronan wrapped an arm around her waist did Blair realize her knees had buckled.

"Let's head back to the Jeep," he said.

Once seated, Blair faced him. "If Ophelia can't reverse the spell, what am I going to do?"

"Keep looking and hoping."

"You're no help."

Chapter Six

AFTER TWO MORE days of living with a mind that refused to be filled in, Blair was willing to try anything. "What if hypnosis doesn't work?" she asked Ronan.

"Then we try something else." He ran a hand down her arm, and his touch soothed her more than she was willing to admit.

"Ms. Murdoch?" asked the assistant who stood at the door leading to Dr. Eleanor Hamilton's office.

"Yes." Blair stood. While she'd never met the therapist, Jackson had some interaction with her and gave her a good recommendation.

"Good luck," Ronan said. "I'll be here when you finish."

She'd thought about asking him into the room, but then she worried she might say something about how attractive she found him, and that would only lead to complications.

Stop obsessing. Blair had already proven to be a bad judge of character. Until her bear decided to make an appearance and help her out, she'd keep her distance from any man.

Dr. Hamilton was small in stature with rather wide hips and short blonde hair. Around fifty, she wore her glasses on a chain around her neck. "Come in and sit down."

After describing how she would conduct the hypnosis, Blair settled back, praying this went well. She remembered the therapist asking her some questions that had nothing to do with the crime, and she somehow ended up talking about lovers and babies. Where had those thoughts come from?

"You can wake up now," the good doctor said.

When the blood rushed back into her body, Blair sat up. How was the session over so fast? They hadn't even talked about the murder. Or had they? "Did I remember anything?"

"I can't be sure. You talked about a man and a woman."

Shit—Jared and his wife she bet. "Anything more about the murder?"

"You spoke about two people arguing."

Yes, she and Jared had gone a round or two after she'd found out that the man of her dreams already had a wife.

"Could the killer have been arguing with Timothy Delahart?" Blair asked. Or did she want to believe she hadn't spilled her guts about that terrible year after she learned Jared wasn't who he claimed to be?

"It's possible. You spoke of someone cheating. Perhaps that was what got Mr. Delahart killed."

"Maybe, since he is a drug dealer—or rather he was a drug dealer." She prayed she hadn't been talking about Jared. When the doctor rose, so did Blair.

"I'm hoping the hypnosis unlocks something in your mind," the good doctor said. "You might start to remember something in a few days."

"Thank you."

When Blair stepped back into the waiting room, Ronan jumped up. His hopeful expression made her smile. He wanted her to remember probably more than she did.

"How did it go?" he said as he moved next to her.

"I don't think I remembered anything, but the doctor said I might recall something in a few days."

Her only memory seemed to be about two people arguing. Because that had to be her and her ex-boyfriend—not Timothy Delahart and a female assassin—Blair decided not to mention it.

Recalling anything about Jared had Blair's stomach doing all sorts of tumbling routines, dredging up a bunch of bad memories.

How had she thought Ronan might be anything like her ex? Ronan was open whereas Jared held more secrets than Pandora's Box.

"You up for some dinner?" he asked.

For a second, she hadn't been aware they'd even left the office. "As in a restaurant?"

He smiled, and her insides tumbled. "It's all I know. I've spent my life chasing after criminals and practically lived in my car. Learning to cook was never my thing."

Poor Ronan. What a waste sitting in a car waiting for something to happen. "Do you think it's safe to go out in public?"

"If I'm with you, it will be. We'll go someplace busy, where no one would dare harm you." The twinkle in his eye convinced her she was overreacting.

Ronan was interested in keeping her safe, but he also seemed to want to keep her happy. "How about McKinnon's Pub and Pool?" she asked. "We'll be surrounded by our kind."

"Sounds good to me."

Just driving to a place different than McKinnon and Associates lightened Blair's mood.

"Tell me about the session," Ronan said. "Was it scary, invasive, frustrating, or enlightening?"

All of the above. Needing a moment to collect her thoughts, she glanced over at him and admired his prominent brows, high cheekbones, and full lips.

She then jerked her mind back to the moment. He was hired to stay by her side, not be her lover.

"I was only with the doctor a few minutes, so it was hard to tell. When I couldn't remember much, I think she figured why waste my time and hers, which was why she snapped me out of my hypnosis."

"A short time? You were in there a little over ninety minutes."

What sounded like gunfire exploded within her brain, and she twisted toward him in disbelief. "No, I wasn't."

From Ronan's pinched lips and worried brow, he was telling the truth. "Look around, Blair. The roads are packed—well as packed as

Silver Lake gets. People are getting off work." He tapped the clock on the dashboard.

"It's five thirty? How is that possible?" Oh fuck, her memory loss was happening again. Like a wildfire out of control, she searched for something to put out the blaze, but she couldn't find anything. "I remember talking to the doctor, just not for how long."

He reached out and patted her leg, but that only pissed her off more. She wasn't a child. "That's what hypnosis does to a person— time seems to stand still."

She hoped she hadn't said more than she'd intended to. "If I thought leaving town would help me gain back some control in my life, I'd hop on the next plane."

Ronan pulled into the parking lot of the restaurant, and the familiar site helped calm a few of her nerves.

"Remember, the judge ordered you to stay in town," he said.

"I know, but a girl can dream, can't she?" When she looked over at Ronan, his jaw was set tight, and his beautiful brown eyes had turned dark. What had she said?

"Come on. Let's have something good to eat and forget all about Timothy Delahart and smoking guns."

"I'd like nothing better." When he didn't sound angry, she let out a breath.

Once they were seated, Blair looked around, recognizing only one or two others. For the most part, she was a stranger in this town.

"You look sad," Ronan said.

She returned her attention back to him. "Wistful maybe. I left town when I was seventeen and didn't return until I got the job at the Wellness Center. While it is my hometown, I don't really know anyone anymore."

"Jackson said you spent a good many years at school?"

"Yes. I earned my bachelors and masters degree in physical therapy." She leaned forward on her elbows. "How about we talk about you? I think I've been asked enough questions lately to last me a lifetime."

He held up his hands. "You want to talk about me?" She nodded. "My life is not very interesting."

She doubted that. "Let me be the judge. I do know your dad had issues."

Ronan chuckled. "Issues? The man was a drunk and a gambler, but he wasn't all bad—at least he wasn't until after my mom died of cancer. Once his will to live evaporated, he turned to some pretty bad vices."

"He must have loved her very much." Her parents were like that, though she didn't think her dad would turn to some kind of vice if her mom died. Daniel Murdoch was a strong and proud man. Most likely, he'd throw himself back into helping run the Clan or work full-time at McKinnon and Associates.

"My dad might have loved Mom, but his demons rotted his brain," Ronan said. "Growing up, he was good to us when he had a job, but then he'd lose it and become depressed. Mom would boost him up, and it worked for a while until he lost that job too."

"I can see where that would wear on a person—and his family."

Ronan nodded. "It was hardest on Lexi. She loved Mom so much, and when she died, Lexi took it upon herself to help Dad."

Blair still couldn't believe that Lexi's own father had tried to sell her. "I'm so lucky my parents still have their health, both mentally and physically."

"You aren't kidding."

The waiter stopped by for their order, and since she wanted to have one night to forget it all, she ordered a beer.

"Coffee for me," Ronan said.

She was about to ask him to join her, but then she remembered he was still on the clock. The waiter left and Blair was anxious to hear more about him. "What made you want to become a bounty hunter?"

"It's simple, really. One of my *talents* is that I have an acute sense of smell. Once I get the scent, I can track that person for miles."

Jackson had mentioned something about that. "I bet being in a restaurant where there are so many odors might be nauseating."

Ronan held up a finger. "Ah, but that is where I differ from everyone else. I do smell things like a fresh grilled steak, popcorn, and rich coffee, but somehow my brain translates that odor into a color. I see patterns and can identify who or what it belongs to. Mingling odors are like mixing paints—some pleasant, some not."

Now she was totally fascinated. "You see odors as colors?"

"Yes, your fragrance, for example, is a rich purple with a blend of light pinks, with an occasional swath of green."

She liked that combination. "Is there any reason why I'm not say, yellow with lime green? I do like those colors."

He smiled. "Do you know that no one has ever asked me that question before? I honestly don't know why certain colors are associated with a person." He held up a finger. "However, if your mood plummets or soars, you give off different colors. For example, once when you were afraid, you emitted a color from the gray spectrum. When you had a good memory—like when you spoke of Ophelia—I saw yellow.

"Wow. So you know what a person is feeling by their color?" He nodded. "It's like everyone in the world is a giant mood ring!" Ronan chuckled, and the sound rumbled deep in her body. A woman could get used to that.

"I wish it were that easy. I have to know them well before I learn what each color means. For instance, gray represents fear or tension to you, but it might mean something different to someone else."

He had paid that much attention to her? That was impressive. "When you walked in here just now, surrounded by the scent of beer, peanuts, and French fries, were you blinded by the assortment of colors?" He smiled and heat shot to her core. Not good.

"No. I can control it—usually."

"Wow. What about the general color aura surrounding evil people? Are they black with specks of red or white?" This was rather fun.

"It's not that simple, though men usually have darker colors."

His ability to see colors for scents was a talent she never knew existed. Their drinks arrived, and Ronan sipped his steaming brew, his gaze off to the side as if something struck him.

She let him think. Unfortunately, that allowed her mind to wander too. Finally, she spoke up. "Not that I really want to talk about the case, but do you or Kalan have any idea what kind of person we're looking for? If he comes into my workplace, I want to be ready."

Ronan stroked his beard. "I don't have a profile other than if he's anything like Timothy Delahart, the killer will be overconfident, have genetic makeup similar to ours, and will most likely be a sociopath."

"That hardly narrows it down. Most of the men on the hill are like that."

Ronan leaned closer. "You mean the Changelings?"

"Yes."

Ronan shook his head. "I'm thinking they aren't involved. I chased Delahart for quite some time and am convinced he came to Silver Lake because he found out I was here. When Connor and I ran into him a while back, I managed to gouge up his face pretty badly. He probably wants revenge."

The idea that someone wanted to hurt Ronan reignited her nerves. "I'm glad he's dead then."

Ronan tossed her another quick smile. "So am I."

The waiter returned and took their order. As soon as he left, she leaned forward. "So, what's your best guess as to who might have killed Delahart?"

Ronan shrugged. "I'm thinking Delahart came to Silver Lake a few days ago. He has always been excellent at assessing who would be the most likely to buy or sell drugs. I'm thinking the killer was either less than anxious to part with his money, or else he believed Delahart was cheating him."

The word cheating ricocheted inside her head. Yes. Perhaps she hadn't been babbling about her and Jared when she told the hypnotist about the two people arguing. "The killer was a woman," she blurted. Ronan's laugh lit her up, and this time not in a good way.

"Shh. Why are you laughing?" *At me?*

"Sweetheart, no woman on earth could get the drop on Delahart."

The nickname of sweetheart swirled in her chest and wrapped around her heart, but she pushed the image aside. "But a woman was there."

He sobered quickly. "What do you mean?"

"While I was under hypnosis, I remember hearing two people arguing. One of them was female."

His brows shot up. "If a woman was there, then she must have been with a man. Delahart wouldn't have given a female the time of day."

That made sense. "I could be wrong."

Ronan reached across the table and placed a hand over hers. "You were very brave to undergo hypnosis. Don't fight the memory loss. It will return."

For some reason, having him give her permission not to remember helped. "Thank you."

"So," he said. "Tell me what is it that you do for a living?"

Chapter Seven

ON MONDAY MORNING, Ronan dropped Blair off in front of the Wellness Center so she wouldn't have to walk down the *alley of death*, and she appreciated his thoughtfulness. The crime scene tape that had blocked the alley was gone, which begged the question: had they learned anything from gathering all that evidence? A woman's strand of hair perhaps or maybe even high heel imprints next to the body? Had Blair been right about a female being present? Or had that memory been about her and Jared? Aargh. Why couldn't she just have her memory return?

Blair rounded the corner to head into her office when she spotted someone different at the receptionist desk. Worry grabbed at her. Their usual receptionist, Eve, was never out sick.

The young woman with the short red hair and thick black glasses glanced up. "Hi. May I help you?"

"I'm Blair Murdoch, and I work here." The uniform should have told her that. "What happened to Eve?"

"She's ill. I'm from a temp agency, so I don't know much more than that."

That made sense. "Thanks."

The woman held out her hand. "I'm Cynthia, by the way."

"Nice to meet you, Cynthia," Blair replied, but she didn't have time to chat. Usually she did, but this woman had a strange vibe about her, or else Blair was just antsy about everyone—man or woman. "I hope you have a nice day."

A flash of something Blair couldn't identify skated across the girl's face. Not needing to deal with any more drama, Blair headed into the break room to grab some coffee. Ainsley was there, pouring some for herself.

Her friend looked up and smiled. "Hey." She set down her cup and hugged Blair. "How are you doing?"

"As good as can be expected."

"Any news?" Ainsley asked.

"No." She'd called her good friend and told her about the hypnosis session. "I'm just happy to be back at work. As nice as the safe room is, it's confining."

"I hear you."

"Do you know what happened to Eve?" Blair asked.

"I just called her. She said it was the strangest thing. Last night she'd finished dinner when all of a sudden she could barely stand up."

"Oh my goodness. I hope she's okay. Has she seen a doctor?"

"No, but she will if the symptoms don't subside by tonight."

"I wonder if Ronan will let me visit her."

Ainsley shook her head. "Jackson would say no."

"Ugh. As much as I love my brothers, having him, Ronan, and Kalan all tell me what to do is wearing thin."

Ainsley rubbed her arm. "You know it's for your own good and just for a short time."

"Let's hope."

Ainsley and Blair stepped back over to the coffee machine. While Ainsley added some cream to her drink, Blair poured herself a cup.

"Speaking of Ronan, how is that going?"

No one else was in the room. Blair sighed. "I'm so confused."

"About what, hon?"

"It's stupid really. I'm in the middle of a crisis, yet something inside of me is so unsettled."

"Unsettled how?"

"Whenever I see Ronan, I keep wondering if maybe he is my

mate."

Sheer joy lit up Ainsley's face and her eyes grew wide. "Did your bear come out of hiding?"

"Don't I wish? That's the problem. My body reacts to him like nothing I've ever experienced, but my bear is still silent. Most likely, it's all this stress that has thrown my body off kilter."

"Oh, hon. Maybe not. This could be it. You know what they say? Your mate comes along when you least expect it."

"You made that up."

"Maybe, but it happened to me and to Lexi."

"But what if he turns out to be another Jared? Without my bear to guide me, I think I should forget about Ronan and keep my distance."

Ainsley cocked her head, "No way. I know both men. They are nothing alike. Even though Ronan is Lexi's brother, Jackson still did a background check on him."

"Doesn't mean he isn't married. I've never asked him."

"Seriously? Do you really think a man like Ronan, one who has been on the go for the last fifteen years, would have a wife?"

"No." For a split second, she wondered if that was why he'd taken the job here—to be near her—his mate. He'd know for sure if they were destined for each other. His wolf wasn't in hibernation.

"There you go. I know how hard it was when you found out about Jared, but now's the time to put that behind you."

"I'd like to."

One of the other workers entered the room, dousing their conversation. "We'll talk later," Blair said.

"Where's Ronan right now?" Ainsley asked.

"He's in the waiting room. I think if I had allowed him, he'd be in the examination room with me and my patients."

Ainsley smiled. "He sounds like Jackson."

Yes, she had always been surrounded by overbearing, protective alpha males, except there was something about Ronan that made her feel that this was more than him just doing a job.

IT WAS CLOSE to lunch, and Ronan was going stir crazy. It wasn't the wait that was getting to him—hell, he'd spent much of his life on stakeout—it was Blair's scent that had his wolf wanting to claw his way out to be close to her. Ronan had to adjust himself whenever she was near. Christ, he hoped she hadn't seen him or else Blair would think he was constantly playing with himself. Geezus, he needed to rein in that damn wolf of his.

Sure, he'd said he could control the colorful images, but not when it came to her. Blair's scent was too powerful, too addicting, too sensual.

Thankfully, this morning hadn't been a total loss. He'd enjoyed watching the patients come in, many with obvious physical issues. When they left, some seemed to have found relief. He liked that. So far, none of the patients had been shifters, convincing him that the killer hadn't found Blair yet.

His cell rang, and Ronan literally jumped. What was up with that? He never let his mental wanderings interfere with his awareness of his surroundings. "Laramie."

"Ronan, it's Kalan. I have the autopsy report for Timothy De-lahart."

Conflicting emotions assaulted him. He wanted to learn the man had suffered greatly, but at the same time he feared the autopsy would somehow implicate Blair. "What did you find?"

"The human doctor said cause of death was loss of blood from the bullet near the throat. The thing is the bullet didn't hit anything vital—at least nothing vital for a shifter."

"That makes no sense. How do you think he really died?"

"That's what I need to investigate," Kalan said. "There were no claw marks and no evidence of any kind of drugs in his system. His fingers were another matter. They were dusted with what might be cocaine or heroin. He might have been testing the drugs to buy them."

"If we can be sure, it might help narrow down the suspect pool."

"You're right, but I'm more hung up on why he died. Have you ever heard of a wolf not being able to heal himself with only a small bullet hole near his throat, especially if no arteries were nicked?"

Because there was no background noise, Ronan figured he was in some kind of soundproof room. No one was within earshot of him either, so Ronan felt comfortable telling him what was on his mind. "It's possible the same witch who stole Blair's memory did something to Delahart." Ronan's mind spun. Sam had claimed the only person capable of erasing a memory would be godlike. He shuddered to think that might be true.

"Did what?" Kalan asked, curiosity filling his voice.

"Maybe he put Delahart into some kind of suspended animation whereby he couldn't heal himself."

"That's a thought, but you know I can't put *that* in my report. Fuck, but this is not going to be a straightforward case. I do hate the ones that involve shifters. I have to be so *creative*."

"Tell me about it. Did the report say anything else?"

"Yes, they found a woman's light auburn hair with gold high-lights on the hem of Delahart's shirt."

Ronan saw a sea of colors—mostly red—and all belonged to him. "We both know Blair was at the crime scene."

"The lab techs are asking for a DNA sample from her."

Fuck. "That will upset her something fierce," Ronan said, though he was sure Kalan was well aware of that.

"I know. Here's the really bad news," Kalan said.

"As if the hair isn't enough?" Ronan's nails sharpened, readying for a fight. "What is it?"

"Delahart was shot from four feet away."

It took a moment for the ramification to sink in. "Meaning there wouldn't have been a struggle between Blair and Delahart in which the gun went off."

"Precisely."

"What are you thinking really went down?" Ronan asked.

"Hell if I know. Nothing is making sense. If Blair weren't my sister, I'd be convinced she killed him. Good thing she doesn't have a motive."

When he worked a case, he'd take any clue, even if it didn't pan out. "Your sister thinks she remembers something."

"What is it?" Kalan asked excitedly.

"She vaguely remembers a man and a woman arguing." Ronan didn't state his opinion for fear of coloring Kalan's.

"Blair thinks a woman killed Delahart? For real?"

Damn. So it was as preposterous as it sounded. "Yes."

"I'll make note of it, but we both know that memories can be deceiving. She might have been thinking of something else."

"True. If Blair tried to help the man, the blood on her shirt makes sense. What I can't figure out is how she got GSR on her hands."

"There's only one explanation. She was framed."

Relief washed away some of his doubt. "I agree."

"I'm thinking the killer would know that by erasing her memory, Blair wouldn't be able to identify him, so he might as well use her as the fall guy by sticking a gun in her hand and firing a shot to misdirect us."

Ronan had considered that possibility too—but only for a moment. "Here's the hole in that theory: most spells wear off with time. Blair is already remembering some things. Why chance it?"

"Then maybe it wasn't a spell."

Ronan struggled to understand what else it could be. "Spells. Curses. Aren't they all the same thing, unless the curse is designed to be unbreakable?" Not that he knew anything about those kinds of things.

"Maybe, but that leads me to wonder who is capable of doing such a thing?" Kalan asked.

Only one option shot to his mind. "Someone from a different realm."

BY THE TIME lunch rolled around, Blair was ready to leave work. All of her patients today had been humans, and even though she had no cause to worry, edginess had worked its way into her psyche.

Relax. I'm safe. Ronan is here to protect me.

After she washed her hands and picked up her purse, she stepped out of her room. As she passed the receptionist's desk, Cynthia's face brightened. "Hi, Blair!"

The strange feeling Blair felt when she'd first met her disappeared. "Hey. How was your first day?"

"Pretty good. Eve has everything so well organized that all I had to do was look at the calendar and point the person in the right direction." She smiled.

"Great." Blair turned to head out to the waiting room to see if Ronan wanted to go to lunch when Cynthia reached out and touched Blair's arm.

"Can I ask you something?" Cynthia asked.

"Sure."

"Since no one else is coming in until two, do you want to go out to lunch together? I live in Crenshaw and don't have the foggiest idea where to go around here."

As much as she appreciated the woman's predicament, Blair thought it odd that she was singled out. "I can't. My boyfriend is here in the waiting room but maybe some other time."

She hadn't meant to say Ronan was her boyfriend, but telling Cynthia he was her bodyguard would cause the new help to ask too many questions.

"Oh. I see. Well, then can you recommend a place?"

"Sure." Blair gave her a couple of recommendations, purposefully omitting Nathan's Pizza since that was where she was going to suggest she and Ronan go.

"Thanks."

Blair walked, or rather rushed, to the waiting room. She tried to tell herself that she was anxious to spend some time outside. In truth, she just wanted to be with Ronan.

Could he be my mate? she asked her sleeping bear.

Damn, why did she bother? For three long years, her inner beast had disappeared. Gone. Poof. It didn't matter how many times she apologized for not listening to her bear when she'd fallen for Jared, her bear was gone for good. Perhaps the worst part was not being able to shift.

Blair stepped into the waiting room. As soon as she appeared, Ronan jumped up. The picture of him naked and on top of her sprang up. Why had that image appeared? Now more than ever, she was convinced that the trauma had more than just erased her memory—it had messed with her sex drive.

Chapter Eight

R ONAN LOVED HEARING about Blair's patients and how she'd helped so many. Because Nathan's Pizza was packed, they weren't able to discuss the case, which was probably for the best.

Blair pushed her plate to the side and tossed her napkin on top. "Lunch was great, but I really need to get back to work."

Ronan pushed back his chair. "I enjoyed our lunch as well."

Her smile came out genuine, and every cell in his body attempted to transform.

Don't you dare shift. Not here, you fool. His damn wolf would be responsible for the end of the shifter secret for good if he appeared.

Thankfully, they left right away, and the bright sunshine and sweet scents helped divert his attention. As they walked back to Blair's workplace, Ronan imagined what it would be like to have Blair in his life for good—safe and happy.

As they passed the alley where the crime occurred, Blair looked over at it. As much as he wanted to ask if anything came to mind, he wouldn't. Tension and anxiety had a way of blocking a memory.

"Would you mind if I asked Jackson to take over for me for a bit?" he asked.

She spun to face him. "No, but why?"

"I want to investigate the alley now that the CSU guys have picked it over."

Her brows creased. "What do you hope to find?"

"I won't know until I find it." He held open the door to her work. "If Jackson is busy, I'll stay."

"You shouldn't have to. I won't run away."

They'd had the conversation a few times. He didn't need to remind her that it was the real killer he was worried about. "I know."

Once Blair slipped into the back, Ronan called Jackson.

"How's my sister?" Jackson asked.

"Good. Say, do you think you could spell me for an hour or so? I need to follow up on a few things."

"Sure. Are you at the Wellness Center?"

"Yes."

"I'll be right there."

True to his word, Jackson showed up ten minutes later. Ronan stood. "I won't be long," he told his friend. "There's something that keeps sticking in my head that I want to check out."

"Care to share?"

"I don't want to jinx it," Ronan said with a smile.

"I understand."

Ronan left, thinking about how Blair had walked out of the side entrance and must have heard Delahart arguing with someone—if her recall during hypnosis was correct. Or had she seen the dead body with the killer standing over him? Blair probably tried to get back inside, but the door had been locked. Trapped, the killer had to do something. Only what? If the shooter had been a witch—or a god—he might have been able to freeze her in place while he erased her memory. If Blair really had been the one to kill Delahart, where was the gun?

Damn. There were too many possibilities.

Once he arrived in the back alley, Ronan began a grid search to look for the shell casing or a possible second bullet. Ronan went on the assumption that Delahart was either dead when Blair came out of the building or had died shortly thereafter. He also wanted to assume that Blair hadn't killed the man. If Ronan had been that killer and a witness was close by, he might put the gun in her hand and pull the trigger in order to leave the GSR residue. That might point a finger at her as being the guilty party.

After twenty minutes, he found no casings or a gun. Damn. The killer was thorough. So what happened in the alley? Only one bullet was found inside Delahart. If Blair hadn't been the one to pull the trigger that killed him, the only way for her to have GSR on her hands was if there was a second bullet somewhere. However, even if Ronan found the shell casing or bullet lodged in stone or dirt that alone wouldn't exonerate her.

As he continued to walk down the alley, a dark blue color floated in front of him. He stopped. While the maroon aspect was gone, he might be in the correct vicinity. Then again, it could be that he was standing next to the dumpster, and those scents had altered some of the colors. The CSU team might have ignored it since it was a good fifty feet from the crime scene. It was always possible the dumpster had been moved since the shooting. It didn't matter. Ronan would check it out anyway.

After another ten-minute search, he hit pay dirt. With a pocket-knife he was never without, he pulled on a pair of thin latex gloves and extracted a bullet from the wall. The question was did it come from the gun that killed Delahart, or had this bullet been there for a while? There was only one way to find out.

He had to let the sheriff's department do their job.

Kalan was at his desk when Ronan arrived. He didn't see Dalton. Using the gloves, Ronan placed the bullet on Kalan's desk.

"Where did this come from?" he asked.

"I found it in a wall by the dumpster behind the Wellness Center."

Kalan pushed it to the side with his pencil. "Looks like the same caliber as the one that killed Delahart."

Ronan's pulse raced. "I'm hoping it will exonerate Blair, instead of implicating her. The person who hit Delahart in the throat had excellent aim. This shot was nowhere near the victim."

Kalan leaned back in his chair and looked up at him. "Implying someone put the gun in Blair's hand?"

"That's my guess."

"You sure you wouldn't rather work here than with Connor?" Kalan said with a small smile.

"Fat chance. Your line of work is too dangerous." Ronan was only kidding, but he enjoyed giving Kalan crap.

"I hear ya. A jury might say that Blair aimed at Delahart, pulled the trigger, and missed. When he moved toward her, she focused, and then shot him again. That bullet stopped him."

"Damn. We're back to square one then."

"Perhaps. Got any other hunches you plan to follow up on?"

"I want to check out Blair's house to make sure the killer hasn't set some kind of trap for her," Ronan said.

"Are you thinking the killer believes Blair's memory will come back, and he plans to silence her for good?"

As much as Ronan didn't like that scenario, it was the most likely one. "Maybe. I still believe the killer is a *special* type of being, but if he's an ordinary warlock, he might return to make sure she keeps quiet."

Kalan sat up and sobered. "Let me know if you find anything."

On his way out, Ronan called Jackson to give him an update. "I should be back in about an hour," Ronan said.

"Take your time. They have good magazines here."

Ronan laughed. Jackson didn't seem the type to enjoy *People* or *Home and Garden.* "You're just happy to be near Ainsley."

"You caught me. Every time Ainsley has a break, she stops out here and chats, so I'm good."

A few minutes later, Ronan turned down Blair's street. As he drew close to her house, he rolled down the window and inhaled the sweet scents. Yellows, greens, and blues swirled in his mind's eye, making him smile. Normally, summer wasn't his favorite time of year, mostly because sitting in a hot car sucked, but today he could appreciate its beauty.

For some reason, he decided to park down the street and go in on foot. He wasn't sure why he didn't pull into the driveway, but his gut was telling him to be cautious.

Once close, he inhaled every few feet to test if anyone was near. When an all too familiar scent teased his nose, his pulse raced and a band around his chest ratcheted tight. Ronan didn't want to believe it could be true.

Needing to make sure he wasn't imagining things, he circled behind Blair's house and cut through the neighbor's yard, not wanting to spook the person.

Slowly withdrawing his weapon, he edged around the house. When his worst fears were confirmed, his hand shook.

"Dad?"

Bill Laramie was kneeling behind Blair's car, his hand under the bumper. He jumped up. "Ronan? Oh, shit. It's not what you think."

"What am I thinking?" His voice sounded as cold as steel.

"I didn't kill that man, I swear."

Ronan ran his gaze up and down his dad's body, not detecting any weapon. He always preached how dangerous firearms were. On the ground sat a white package, looking suspiciously like drugs. Why would his father assume Ronan would think he had anything to do with Timothy Delahart's death? Guilt perhaps? "Move away from the car and tell me what happened."

It didn't matter what his dad said; Ronan was sure he was involved in his nemesis' death somehow. Why else would his father be this far from home? Slipping his phone from out of his pocket, Ronan called Kalan.

"Murdoch."

"You need to get to Blair's. I found our killer."

"Who was it?"

"My dad."

"No way. Are you sure?"

"Do Changelings lie?"

"On my way."

Once Kalan disconnected, Ronan slipped his gun back into his holster and strode toward his father. "I thought I smelled you at the crime scene, but I didn't want to believe it. What are you doing at Blair's?" The answer seemed rather obvious since a packet of drugs was on the ground next to him.

"I swear I'm innocent."

Ronan laughed, but it held no joy—only disgust and bitterness. "You stopped being innocent once I turned ten. Tell me what happened."

"I know it looks bad."

"It looks criminal."

"Okay, you know how I have a tendency to gamble?" Ronan refused to comment. "Anyway, I was losing big when this dame comes up and says she wants to sit in on our game. I couldn't turn her down, you know what I mean? Women don't know shit about cards."

Ronan wanted to haul off and smack his old man for his sexist attitude, but it wouldn't do any good. The man was incorrigible. Hell, he'd already tried to sell his own daughter. "Go on," he said.

"Bitch turned out to be some kind of card shark. I lost five G's that night."

"Money you didn't have," Ronan added.

"True, but she said if I'd help her with one little deal, we'd be clear."

Ronan could figure out the rest. "This little deal involved doing a drug deal and killing the buyer."

His father held up his hands. "No. I mean yes, but not the killing part. I may be a drunk and a gambler, but I ain't no killer."

"Desperate men do desperate things."

"You don't understand."

"Enlighten me." He was fast losing his patience. "Run through exactly what went down."

"We were just supposed to sell drugs to some guy by the name of Delamont or Delaspot or something."

"Delahart…"

"Yeah, that's it. My partner had the drugs. I was there to be the muscle in case he hassled her."

"Her? What was her name?" Well, shit. Blair was right.

"Darinda. Didn't catch her last name, but she was a looker all right."

He couldn't have cared less. "Go on."

His dad shoved a hand through his messy hair and chewed the inside of his cheek—a habit that Ronan had always disliked. "Well, she gives the drugs to the guy and takes his payment. I think it's a done deal when, all of a sudden, this chick comes out of the side entrance of some building and sees us."

Blair. Ronan's fangs sharpened, and his bones cracked. "She must have been surprised." Ronan was pleased that he was able to keep his tone even.

"Boy, was she. I grabbed the girl so she wouldn't get away and scream her pretty little head off when Darinda pulled a gun and shot the guy. That was not part of the plan, but since he was a shifter, I didn't think much of it. But then the guy didn't move."

"Why was that?"

"Fuck if I know."

"What did the girl do?"

"She didn't do anything. She just stared and stuff."

That didn't make any sense. Blair would have tried to save De-lahart. "She didn't scream?"

"No. I thought she was in shock or something. Then Darinda hands me the gun and tells me to put it in the girl's hand and fire a shot."

Everything made sense now. "So you snatch the drugs and the money and take off," Ronan said, filling in the blank.

"Not then I didn't. I figured that Darinda would stiff me, so when she was helping the girl back to her car, I stole two small packets of the drugs and then stuffed it under the girl's bumper. I put some of the money in my pocket."

"How did this Darinda know which one was Blair's car?'

"I don't know."

Sirens sounded, a car door closed, and seconds later, Kalan and his partner Dalton Garner showed up.

"Ronan, are you okay?" Kalan said as he rushed up to him.

"Yes, I'm fine."

"You don't look fine."

Ronan didn't understand his concern. Dalton cuffed his father. "Why are you here?"

"What do you mean? You called me and said you'd found Delahart's killer. That it was your dad."

"I don't remember that."

Kalan studied him. "I think you need to come with me," Dalton clasped Ronan's arm, but he shook him off.

"I'm good. I need to get back to Blair. Jackson's with her, and I told him I'd return in an hour."

"Let me worry about Jackson."

Kalan never lied. As Ronan watched Dalton lead his father away, Kalan pulled out his phone and took pictures of the drugs and money. He then made a call. "If you want to follow Dalton back to the precinct, go ahead. I need to wait here for the crime scene unit to process these drugs."

"Drugs?"

"Ronan, what the hell is wrong with you?"

"Nothing."

His friend moved closer. "You called me and said your dad had killed Delahart. The caller ID said it was your phone, and I recognized your voice."

Oh, shit, he didn't remember even making the call. A feeling of dread bigger than the sea flowed through him. "Are you sure?" It was a stupid question. He pulled out his phone, and sure as shit, the sheriff's department number was the last one called.

"Of course, I'm sure."

"Then I think we're dealing with something a lot bigger than some big, bad witch."

Chapter Nine

"**W**HERE'S RONAN?" BLAIR asked Jackson during one of her breaks. His long legs were stretched halfway into the main area.

He put down the magazine he was reading and shrugged. "He said he needed to do something and would be back in an hour. Problem is it's been closer to two now."

"That's not like him." *I think.* "Maybe I should give him a call to make sure he's okay."

Jackson chuckled. "You just want to get your Ronan fix."

Shit. Her face heated. "So not true. I'm worried he found out something that I won't like."

"Be in denial."

Not needing grief from her older brother, Blair headed back to the break room to call Ronan, thankful the room was empty. Sometimes it was hard to find privacy at work.

"Hey," Ronan said, sounding rather strange.

"Is everything okay? Jackson said you weren't going to be gone long."

"Yeah, I'm sorry. I should have been back sooner, but something happened—something not good."

Worry crushed her. Ronan sounded distant, and possibly frightened. She waited for him to elaborate, but he didn't. "What happened?"

"I'm not sure."

Blair stepped over to the table and sat down. "What do you mean you're not sure?" She remembered using those same words when she'd called Kalan that first time. Ronan then explained why he went to her house. As much as she didn't like to think the real killer was still around and might want to harm her, she understood his logic.

"I remember sneaking in through the neighbor's yard in order to enter around the side of your house."

"Did you see or sense someone?" He claimed he had an unusually high sense of smell.

"Yes. I remember seeing my dad crouched down behind your car, and then it was as if time stood still. Next thing I knew, Kalan was there arresting him."

"What?" Too many questions bombarded her at once.

"Which part is the shocker? The idea that time stood still or that my dad was arrested?"

She wasn't able to process any of it. "Both."

"Neither makes sense to me either. Nothing like this has ever happened to me before. I'm aware of my surroundings one minute, and the next I'm somewhere else. I'm scared, Blair. I can't remember a damn thing!"

Her heart plummeted. "Do you think someone erased your memory too?"

"It seems to be the only explanation."

Sympathy swamped her. "I know how you feel."

"I'm sure you do. As much as I hate that you went through the same thing, I feel a bit better knowing I didn't just have some brain fart."

Her mind swam. When the blood stopped pounding in her head, she focused on the here and now. "What are you going to do?"

"I'm hoping my father can clear up a few things. After Kalan and Dalton arrived, they had to arrest Dad since he was taking drugs out from under your back bumper."

What felt like a bolt of lightning struck her, nearly frying her nerves. "Drugs? In my car?"

"No one is claiming they're yours. If my father knew they were there, maybe he planted them."

Her mind grappled with that news. "I'm not sure they won't think I'm responsible. If I were a cop, I'd assume I stashed them in my car for safekeeping. The plan might have been for my partner to come to my house to pick them up." Shit, this was getting worse by the moment.

"Don't think like that."

Easy for him to say. "Will they question me again? It's not like I can tell them anything."

"I'm heading over to the station now to see what Dad has to say and to ask Kalan that exact question."

"Call me if you learn anything." Her voice cracked.

"Will do."

As soon as she disconnected, the new girl, Cynthia, came into the room. "Blair? Are you okay?" she asked.

She blew out a breath and looked up at her. "Yes. I'm fine." *Not at all.*

"Mrs. Wellington is here for her appointment and has been waiting."

Oh shit. She'd forgotten about her. "Thanks."

If all this mess didn't clear up soon, no telling what would happen to her.

"I WANT TO speak with my father," Ronan told Detective Dalton Garner.

Dalton held up his hand. "He's being processed, but once we're finished, you can see him." Dalton motioned for Ronan to take a seat. "How about telling me what happened back there at Blair's house?"

Ronan wanted to pace, but if he did, that might agitate his animal more than it already was. He told Dalton how he'd wanted to make sure no one was at Blair's house. "Because she remembered nothing, one of our theories is that someone put a spell or curse on her—one that might wear off with time. If that were the case, this witch or warlock would want to make sure Blair didn't talk."

"And you thought this witch might be at her house to sabotage Blair or worse kill her?"

"It was a thought."

Dalton dragged a hand down his clean-shaven chin. "Based on what evidence?"

Ronan leaned closer and lowered his voice. "Some *people* don't leave evidence, if you get my drift." Especially if there were goddesses involved, but he wasn't about to make that statement where someone could overhear.

Dalton nodded, seeming to understand that he was speaking about some kind of supernatural entity. "Have you consulted with Ophelia about this? Maybe she can reverse it."

"We have. All she said was that Blair was in danger."

"Then what happened at the house?"

"Then nothing—it's all a blank." Ronan leaned back. "It's like what happened to Blair. As soon as you and Kalan arrived, I seemed to snap out of whatever was creating the time warp and memory loss. I could hardly believe it when you told me that I'd said my dad was the killer." Ronan tugged on his beard and twisted the end to a point—a nervous habit that drove Lexi crazy.

Dalton picked up a worn pencil on his desk. "You don't think that's true anymore?"

"I don't think anything. That's the point." He'd nearly shouted. "But I must have figured out something or I wouldn't have called Kalan for backup. I'm convinced some very powerful witch or goddess ripped the memory right out of my head," he whispered, not able to control his frustration anymore.

Dalton's grip on the pencil tightened. "Goddess?" he mouthed.

"Yes. My dad's no warlock, so it had to be someone who's not from around *here*."

"Did this person float above you like Vinea used to do?"

"How the fuck would I know? Especially if he or she had been invisible, and I also don't remember detecting any kind of scent." He told Dalton how Blair thought she remembered a man and woman arguing.

Dalton held up his hands. "Okay. I get it. Look, it will take some time to process your dad. Why don't you check up on Blair, and I will contact you when you can speak with your father?"

Ronan wasn't anxious to see him, but he of all people might be able to tell whether his dad was lying. "I'll do that."

Before he stood, an officer he didn't recognize barreled down the hallway and aimed straight at them. Dalton nodded at the man. "What did Mr. Laramie say?"

"That he was innocent, of course. He's in Silver Lake to visit his kids, and swears he had nothing to do with any drugs or murder."

Dalton glanced over at Ronan. "Was your dad down here to see you two?"

"Hell no. Remember, my dad tried to sell my sister. He knows there will be no warm welcome for him here. We broke ties with him after the stunt he pulled with that gambler, Justin Kapok. Besides, I'm sure Lexi never gave him her address, and I know I sure as hell didn't."

"He could have done a little research."

"His brain is so pickled, I'm not sure he even knows what a search engine is."

"Could he have hired someone to track you down?" Dalton asked. "Maybe he wants to make amends, like he claims."

Ronan wasn't buying it. "My dad is a drunk and a gambler. I'm surprised he had enough money to get down here, let alone hire a private investigator. Do we know if he drove or flew?"

The newcomer glanced over at Dalton. "I didn't ask him."

"Are you finished processing him?" Dalton asked with some irritation.

"For now. The lab did a quick check on the drug package he

had, and the contents are identical to what was found on Delahart's fingers."

Fuck. What had his dad gotten himself into?

Dalton pushed back his chair. "You might as well come in with me. He might be more willing to talk if you're there."

Ronan huffed out a laugh. "You don't know my father."

Ronan stood, steeling himself for the unpleasant confrontation. His dad did have drugs in his possession, so he'd do time for sure. The question was would it also be for murder?

When Ronan entered the small interrogation room, his dad's scent nearly blinded him. The brown was deep and pulsating, and the red and blue more intense than usual. His dad was scared—as well he should be.

"Son?"

"Dad." It was difficult for Ronan to even look at the man. Gambling had caused him nothing but problems. Despite Ronan paying for a treatment center a few years ago, his father had slipped right back into the addiction.

"Sir, can you tell us what happened?" Dalton asked.

He shrugged his shoulders. "I was walking by some alley when I heard this altercation."

"Which alley?" Dalton asked.

"I'm not sure. I only just arrived in town and don't really know my way around."

His father never did have the best memory, sober or not.

"Go on," Dalton prodded.

"I heard a gunshot. When I looked in the direction of the sound, this woman was half dragging another woman down the alley. At first, I thought she might have been shot, but I didn't see any blood. Not wanting anyone to spot me, I hid in a doorway. The second woman—a redhead—seemed really out of it, but I could see the first lady had two canvas bags with her. She set them down behind the car so she could help the girl into the driver's side." His dad looked off to the side. "I kind of needed some cash, so I snuck up behind the car, stuck my hand in the bag and grabbed two small packages and some cash. When the car door closed, I jammed the packages under the bumper and stuffed some of the money in my pockets." His dad looked over at him. "You believe me, son, right?"

The brown scent was there, but the red and blue had shifted to maroon and black, implying some of his story was true and some was false. Only which part was which? "I haven't decided yet."

"It's the truth, I swear."

All imprisoned men claimed they were innocent. "Why are you in town?" Ronan asked.

"To see you and Lexi."

"Do you really think she wants to see you after you tried to sell her to that scum?"

His father looked away, his colors changing to a deeper brown. From the increased level of fear the man was experiencing, he was trying to come up with another explanation.

"I thought it was worth a try."

"How were you able to afford to come down here? And how did you know where she lived?"

The man's colors turned almost black. Gotcha!

Dalton took over the interrogation from there, but his father kept insisting he was innocent. Finally, even Dalton must have realized that questioning him wasn't getting them anywhere. "We caught you with the drugs, Mr. Laramie. You'll be in here for a long time," Dalton announced.

"I took drugs from a drug dealer. Is that so bad?"

Ronan pushed back his chair and stormed out, too disgusted to hear more.

DARINDA WAS TOTALLY pissed. Bill Laramie was an idiot who couldn't be trusted. It was partly her fault. She'd left the drugs and money for him to take, thinking if he was found with the goods, he'd be accused of the murder. And now he had been caught. The big question was whether he would try to implicate her?

Sure, Darinda could never be held captive. She'd nod and disappear, but her status in the dark realm would be far less if she were ever caught. Androf would not be pleased, especially when a manhunt—or more accurately a goddess hunt—ensued. The solution to this dilemma was easy enough though.

One second she was in her hotel room—because sleeping in a real bed was the one perk of this job—and the next she was in the interrogation room. She hovered in the corner for a second to make sure that Dalton or Ronan didn't return. What a shame Ronan had a mate. She would have enjoyed dicking around with him. Shifter diversions were always so much fun. She wouldn't be stupid like Vinea had been and let herself be caught by a goddess of the light. Shame on her. And Devon? Vinea had been so weak around that man. Darinda knew better than to let any man get to her.

Darinda materialized, and Bill Laramie practically fell out of his chair. "What are you doing here? How did you get in?" he stammered.

"Bill, Bill, Bill. Surely, you've figured out by now that I'm a goddess."

He practically drooled on himself. "A goddess? I had no idea." Something close to a smile appeared on his face. "So that was how you beat me at cards. I knew that no human woman could have done that."

What an ass, but she did like his style. "I didn't have to use any magic to beat you. You have more tells than the U.S. Mint has coins."

He folded his arms over his chest. "What do you want? I told them all about you. They'll find you, you know."

Darinda laughed. "You only told your son—kind of—and I erased his memory. But if they do find me, I'll just disappear."

He visibly shook. "What do you want?"

"I want you to retract your statement."

"Re-retract?"

"Yes, that means to take back."

He shoved back his chair. "I know what it means, bitch."

Darinda disappeared and pressed down on his shoulders, forcing him to sit again. She then appeared across from him. "Now listen, asshole. You are going to do exactly as I say, or you won't live past tomorrow. Do I make myself clear?"

To prove that she was fully capable of providing a lot of pain, she focused her gaze on his chest and squeezed. His hand covered his heart and his eyes bugged out. "Yes, yes. Now stop it."

"I'm going to tell you what to say. You never should have spilled the beans to your son. It was why I had no choice but to erase his memory."

"If you're so powerful, why didn't you stop me from talking in the first place?"

Darinda looked off to the side. "I was busy. I can't be two places at once. Otherwise, I would have made sure you didn't talk. I don't need anyone to know that I was even there."

"So you want me to say I organized the drug sale and then shot Delahart?"

"Yes."

He shook his head. "Lady, that's way above my pay grade. I never could have pulled that off. You saw that I had no money. How could I have purchased the drugs in the first place?"

Damn. She was slipping. Darinda had thought she'd figured everything out. "Tell them most of the truth—that you had an accomplice—but say you killed Delahart."

"What do you care if you're charged with murder or not?" he asked. "You said they can't catch you."

"I don't need my boss learning I had anything to do with that man's death." She released her hold on him. "Now here is what you're going to say."

Chapter Ten

R ONAN NEEDED TO get his head on straight before he faced
Blair. It hadn't helped that his memory had either been stolen
or blocked, shaking him to the core, or that he had to sit through an
interview with his dad and watch the man lie through his teeth. Too
many times he found himself wanting to strangle his father, but his
pity for the shell-of-a-man had surfaced in time. Dad was sick, and
mentally ill people often made poor choices.

Needing to see, touch, and smell his mate in order to center
himself again, Ronan headed on back to the Wellness Center. When
he rushed in, Jackson was on his phone. He nodded then held up a
finger. "Sure thing, thanks." He disconnected. "How did it go?" he
asked.

"I'm not sure where to begin." No one was in the waiting room,
so Ronan sat next to him. He explained about finding another bullet,
but that it might not even belong to the gun that shot Delahart.
"After I turned in the bullet to Kalan, I headed on over to Blair's."
He then explained why he wanted to check out her place. "When I
arrived, I found my dad crouched down behind Blair's car."

"Your dad?"

"Yup. Can you believe it? After that, it's just blank."

"What do you mean it's a blank?" Jackson asked.

"I believe the same thing that happened to Blair, happened to
me."

Jackson leaned back in his seat and glanced to the ceiling. He then sat up straighter. "I think we need to call Vinea."

"What do you think the former goddess can tell us?"

"I'm not sure, but she might know of someone who has the talent to erase minds."

"I agree it has to be a god or goddess, but hasn't Vinea been out of the biz, so to speak, for some time?"

"Yes, for ten months, but that is a drop in the bucket when you consider she lived in the dark realm for centuries. All I'm saying is that she might know who has this *talent* of erasing memories."

"It can't hurt to call her."

As soon as Jackson connected with Vinea, he stood and paced the length of the small waiting room, while he explained the situation. Much of the time Jackson nodded and said he understood.

He finally disconnected and returned to his seat. "Vinea was very helpful. She said that each of the goddesses and gods have different *talents*. One goddess, by the name of Darinda, has been to Silver Lake before. Her specialty is erasing memories. Vinea wouldn't be surprised if Darinda targeted Silver Lake to get back at her. In fact, they had a little competition going for a few hundred years. Apparently, Vinea was the boss' pet, at least for a while, and Darinda always hated her for it."

He could follow the thinking. "Since we're associated with McKinnon and Associates, this would be a good way to get back at Vinea, to show how much power this dark goddess now has."

"Exactly."

His mind whirled, the pieces fitting together nicely. "When Blair underwent hypnosis, she remembered hearing a male and female argue. It's possible this goddess, Darinda, argued with my dad or Delahart, and that's what Blair remembered." For the first time in days, a rush of endorphins recharged him. "Do you have any idea how we can contact this dark goddess?"

"Are you kidding? We don't contact her. She has to come to us."

Ronan didn't want to think what damage an immortal could inflict on them. "How do we combat her if she does show up?"

"You can't. They're freaking immortal. Let's hope she's had her fun, aka revenge, and is on her way down under," Jackson said.

Ronan didn't like the odds. "But what if she wants to make sure Blair and I never remember?"

Jackson lifted his shoulders. "If a goddess is responsible, I doubt your memory will ever return, so you might not have to worry."

"Probably true, which means we can't hurt her." Damn. Humans and shifters didn't stand a chance against a goddess. His cell rang. "It's Kalan," he told Jackson. "Yes?"

"Your father just confessed to killing Delahart and to setting up Blair."

It was as if someone punched him in the stomach. "What? I just left the interview. He said he was innocent—more or less."

"I read the transcript when I returned in order to learn what he'd told you and Dalton. A few minutes ago, he called us in and said he'd made it all up."

"I see. I think there may be more to this than meets the eye, but we need to discuss it in private."

"Fine by me. In the meantime, I'm going to get the charges dropped against my sister."

That was the only good news he'd had all day. "That's great. Would you mind if I meet with my dad? I think he might tell me why he changed his story so fast."

"Be my guest."

"Thanks." He turned to Jackson. "Can you give me another hour?"

"For Blair, you can have all day."

Ronan told him what Kalan said and how the charges would be dropped. "Do you want to give Blair the good news?"

"I can, but if that goddess is out there, Blair might be in more danger than ever before."

"Well, fuck. Darinda might want to tie up loose ends for various reasons—revenge, pride, her hatred for Vinea, to name a few—and we're caught in the crosshairs. Did Vinea say if Darinda is vying for her old job?" Ronan asked. "She has to know Vinea isn't returning, right?"

"Vinea didn't mention it, but how can Darinda not know? She is a goddess after all."

Jackson made sense. "It's possible that this Darinda person has nothing to do with all of this killing and memory loss. We just don't know." The frustration bit at him.

"True, but if I recall correctly, Vinea once told me the dark realm has some level of status associated with not getting caught. If Darinda's name is bandied about, it will cause a stir both here and in her realm. She'll want to avoid that. I've heard their boss, Androf, is not exactly the forgiving type."

That almost boosted his mood. "Maybe I should take an ad out in the paper then and address it to Androf."

Jackson flashed him a smile. "Be careful. If she isn't involved, she may decide to become so, and you guys would be as good as dead."

"I can't let that stop me from trying to learn the truth. Hopefully, I won't be gone too long. I know you want your life back."

"Be careful."

"Will do." Needing to clear his head, Ronan decided to walk to the sheriff's department. The ten-minute stroll would give him time to calm down. It probably didn't matter what his dad claimed was the actual truth; he'd still be spending many years in jail. Still, Ronan wanted to understand why he'd changed his mind. Ronan needed confirmation whether or not Darinda was behind all of this—or some other unnamed person.

When Ronan entered the sheriff's department, Kalan was at his desk. He glanced up and then stood. "Ready to see your dad?"

"Yes."

"I had him escorted to a private room so the two of you can talk. There will be a guard outside the door in case he tries something."

That wasn't necessary—or so he hoped. "Thanks."

"We'll talk when you're done."

Kalan escorted him to a room where his dad was sitting at a

table, cuffed. He looked worse than an hour ago, if that was possible. As soon as Kalan closed the door, Ronan studied the man. "Why did you lie?"

"When?"

"When Dalton and I interrogated you about where you got the drugs?" Ronan asked.

His dad looked off to the side. "No use copping to something I didn't do."

"If that's the case, why change your story?"

"Had to."

"Did Darinda threaten you?" Ronan asked.

His father jerked so hard, Ronan thought Darinda might have hit him. "Darinda? So you do remember what I told you at that woman's house. You sure as hell didn't say anything when that other fellow was in here."

"It was your story to tell." Ronan was pleased with that comeback. His father must not be aware that Ronan's memory had been erased and hadn't returned. "To be honest, I was in such shock to find you at Blair's house that I might have forgotten a few of the details. Would you do me the courtesy of going over it again?"

"I don't see the point. You can't tell anyone about a goddess. They'll think you're crazy." He looked to the ceiling. "Though, death is preferable to a life in prison."

"Dad, come on."

"Don't got that long to live anyway. I found out about two months ago that I have liver cancer."

"Cancer? How long do you have?" Something small twitched in his chest. Ronan might not have any love left for this man, but as a human being, he did have compassion and wouldn't wish that disgusting disease on anyone.

"A few months. I kept hoping my wolf would heal me, but it's no good. I drank too much."

"I'm sorry. Can you tell me again what happened? The least you can do is make this right in your life."

Ronan tried to hide his emotions as his dad told him about Blair witnessing Darinda shooting Delahart. When his dad mentioned how he'd put the gun in Blair's hand and shot the weapon, it took all of Ronan's control not to jump across the table and punch him.

The story filled in all the blanks that had been plaguing him. Ronan hoped that by detailing what went down to Blair, she might recall some of it too. At least now he didn't need to remember what his dad said at Blair's house. "This goddess will figure out you took some of the drugs. Do you think she'll try to contact you?"

"She already did," his father said as he looked away.

Ronan's fists tightened. "When?"

"About half hour ago. She just appeared in the room and said if I told anyone about her, she'd kill me. Then the more I thought about it, the more I liked the idea."

Ronan glanced around the room, wishing Vinea still lived in Silver Lake. She would be able to tell where Darinda was right now. Though, if she were in this room, she could erase even more of his memory. Thankfully, this conversation was being recorded. Ronan stood. "I'm sorry this happened."

His dad's eyes were watery. "Do you think I could see Lexi one more time?"

He'd been about to say when hell froze over, but it was his sister's decision. She might have something to say to him so that she would have closure on everything. "I'll ask her."

When Ronan stepped from the room, he couldn't decide if he was better off knowing the truth or not. Having confirmation that a goddess was responsible for what happened really pissed him off and scared him to death at the same time.

Kalan was on the phone when Ronan returned. He scribbled something down and then hung up. "Well?"

"We need privacy," Ronan said. He couldn't talk about the goddesses with the whole precinct nearby.

"How about joining me and Dalton in the interrogation room?"

Once the three of them were seated in the stuffy, incredibly offensive smelling room where colors were everywhere, Ronan clasped his hands together and gripped hard.

"Tell me what you found out," Dalton said.

Ronan explained about Jackson's call to Vinea, and then about his conversation with his dad.

"You're saying that goddess from the dark realm lured your dad down to Silver Lake, killed Delahart, framed Blair, and erased both of your memories?"

"Yup."

"Then when your dad denied any wrong doing, she appeared in his cell and told him if he didn't confess that she'd kill him?"

"That's right."

Dalton tapped his pencil on the table. "Your dad's confession makes proving his guilt unnecessary and exonerates Blair, so things can be neatly wrapped up, but why does Jackson think you and Blair are still in danger? Even if we could find this Darinda, and managed to lock her up, she'd just disappear and cause total chaos."

"I agree. Jackson thinks it has something to do with pride as well as revenge against Vinea."

Kalan raised his brows. "The revenge part I get, but why pride?"

Ronan explained about how important it was for gods and goddesses not to get caught. "Their boss, Androf, looks down on it. It means they are less than worthy in his eyes."

"So, by taking out Blair, and possibly you, no one other than your dad can rat her out, and he won't unless he's willing to die."

"Precisely. The fact we both work for Devon's family makes us particularly juicy targets. What I don't understand is shouldn't Androf be aware of what went down already? If he doesn't, what kind of god is he?

"You're asking the wrong guy." Dalton stabbed a hand through his hair. "What if this goddess does come after you?"

That was the question that kept rattling in his head. "I need to figure out a way to fight her."

"And how do you think that will end?"

"Badly."

Kalan waved a finger. "Talk to Missy's mate, Zane. He is from another realm, one called Cargonia. He said he ended up on Earth after he killed a demon by cutting off its head. That might work on a goddess too. He was an expert swordsman as well as a maker of swords. If anyone can take down a goddess, he can."

"I'll speak to him, but I can't ask him to follow us around for the next few months. I imagine Darinda will strike when we're alone."

"Probably true, but he might be able to teach you the art of wielding a sword."

Ronan would enjoy learning another fighting technique. "I'll do that. I refuse to take any chances with Blair's life though. I plan on keeping a close eye on her."

A small smile lifted Kalan's lips. "Are you sure that's all you'll be doing?"

Damn. He knew. "You could tell?"

"Tell? Yeah. I'm surprised Blair hasn't mentioned that the two of you are mates. Growing up, she talked about what her mate would be like, and you fit the picture, right down to the beard. She really is a romantic, you know."

His wolf sat up and howled. *She likes our looks!*

To be honest, Ronan hadn't seen her romantic side, but he could understand why he hadn't. Blair had her memory yanked and then was arrested for murder. Something like that would put a damper on anyone's libido—including her bear's.

"I'm sure when things calm down, we'll discuss it—assuming we live that long," Ronan said. "Right now, we have more pressing things to talk about—like some goddess out for revenge. When will Blair officially be released?" He looked over at Dalton.

"The judge will return to town tomorrow, and I'll have him sign the papers then, but consider it a done deal."

Ronan stood and shook both of their hands. "Thank you," Ronan said.

"No, thank you. You figured it out," Dalton said.

"With help from Vinea and my dad. I'd like to meet her some-day. She sounds like an interesting lady."

Both men smiled. "She is at that," Kalan said.

Chapter Eleven

B LAIR SENSED THE moment Ronan walked into the Wellness Center building. Dare she hope her bear was finally waking up? If Ronan were her mate, she would hope her bear would want to meet him.

No matter how many times she convinced herself it was only a matter of time before her bear surfaced, hope was slowly seeping out of her when she didn't make her presence known.

Wake up, dammit. What is it going to take?

Maybe Blair should speak to Ophelia about her problem. Or not. Then she'd have to confess why her bear had gone into hiding in the first place—and Blair wasn't ready to share that humiliation with anyone other than Ainsley.

It was probably wishful thinking that she and Ronan were mates. When Blair had questioned her brother earlier about where Ronan had gone, Jackson said he'd received a call from Kalan about something and would be back shortly.

Her last patient had left fifteen minutes ago. It was time to go. She was cleaning up when a knock sounded on her door. It was Ronan. She was sure of it. Her hands shook as a sizzle of excitement raced up her body. *Help me*, she pleaded to her bear. *Is he the one? Don't you want to know?*

Perhaps she wasn't ready to act on her feelings. She had a murder charge over her head and needed to focus on that.

After running her hands down her shirt and then pulling out her hair tie, Blair yanked open the door. She was going to be her usual distant self, but when she saw Ronan smiling, something inside her snapped. Heat suffused her body, and her breath lodged in her throat.

Mate, mate. Blair froze. Had she thought that, or had her bear finally awoken?

"Come in."

"I have some good news and some not so good news," he said as he raked his gaze over her and inhaled. Did her colors change being so close to him? Could he tell she was turned on despite the blanket of depression that she'd been wrapped in these last few days?

Blair should probably suggest they leave the office right now and have Ronan tell her the news on the way, but her tongue wouldn't work. All she could think about was taking off his clothes.

Where had that idea come from? *Bear, are you there?*

"What is it?" she asked once she shut off her libido. He was still smiling so it had to be good news.

"We found the killer. You're a free woman."

The relief was so great that she threw herself into his arms. As much as she wanted to kiss him, at the last second, she lowered her face to his shoulder. His scent entered on the next inhale, and it took all of her effort not to press closer against him. A bit embarrassed by her uncharacteristic reaction, Blair stepped back and looked up at him. "How?"

Ronan stepped around her and then faced her. "My dad confessed."

"Your dad confessed? I'm confused."

Ronan told her everything what had happened from the time she walked out of the building and seeing Darinda with a gun in her hand, to when his dad had put that same gun in her hand and shot it.

"So your father framed me?"

"I believe it was Darinda's doing. My dad is a lot of things, but he's not very creative, nor is he a killer."

"Then why did he confess?"

"Because Darinda is a goddess, and—"

"A goddess?" Her mind swam with what that meant. "So that explains the memory loss, and why even Ophelia couldn't retrieve my memories."

"That's what I was thinking," Ronan said.

"Wait a minute. If this Darinda person shot Delahart, why use a gun? Surely, she can kill with just a look."

Ronan shrugged. "I don't know. She probably didn't want the world to know she was a goddess. It seems as if the bullet might have been a misdirect. It didn't kill Delahart. Something else did."

"How did you find this out?"

"Darinda appeared to my father when he was in the holding cell, and she threatened him. If he didn't confess, she'd kill him. And we know she can, even in a jail cell."

"Bloody hell!" She didn't know a lot about his dad, but from what she'd learned how he'd treated Lexi, Blair wasn't too sad he would be incarcerated for a long time. However, he had at one point, alongside his wife, helped in raising Ronan become the man he was today. "So he'd rather confess than have Darinda kill him."

"My dad told me he has cancer and doesn't have long to live anyway. Even though he confessed, he came clean with me. He decided he wanted a swift end."

Her chest practically vibrated from the pain Ronan must be feeling. If that wasn't a sign they were mates, she didn't know what was. Too bad Ronan never acted as if he was interested in her.

"I'm sorry."

"Me too.

"How about we get out of here?" she said. "I'm thinking a good run around the lake to release some of this built up tension from the past few days might do both of us some good." She didn't say whether they would be in human or animal form, since she hadn't been able to shift since her bear had deserted her.

Blair just said that to entice him there. It would give her the chance to tell him the truth. If the truth didn't free her, nothing would.

Or maybe some good hard loving would do the trick. She couldn't help but smile at that thought.

He studied her for a moment. "I can't think of anything I'd like better."

Just thinking about seeing Ronan naked had her body heating.

Ronan escorted her to his Jeep. For the first time in a long while, he wasn't scoping out the neighborhood. Once he pulled onto the street, her thoughts cleared. "Do you think this goddess Darinda will just go back to the dark realm now that she's finished her assignment?" she asked.

"I wish I knew."

She slumped back in her seat. "I wonder if Vinea can find out anything."

"Jackson has already called her. She was the one who gave him Darinda's name in the first place. Besides, Vinea's in no state to travel anywhere far—even when in her invisible state."

"Oh no, I wasn't suggesting she go to the dark realm. I was just wondering if she could establish a mental link with the woman. I don't believe all of her powers are gone."

He glanced over at her. "You have such faith in people. I like that, but I doubt we could believe anything Darinda says. If Vinea could contact her, it might make Darinda want to cause her even more undue stress."

"You're right. I wasn't thinking clearly."

He reached out and briefly squeezed her hand, sending her thoughts spiraling. A few minutes later, they turned down the road leading to the lake. She hadn't been there since…when? Too long ago.

Ronan parked. "Ready for me to run circles around you?" He grinned, and heat rushed to between her legs.

Perhaps she wasn't ready to tell all. Would he even believe her if she said she hadn't been able to shift in almost three years?

Coward. Once more, she wasn't sure where that thought came from. "We'll see about that."

The air was warm and surprisingly dry for July. The slightly hazy overcast skies would make this the perfect day to play—or to confess her sins. As they walked down the path, she imagined taking off her clothes, all the while trying to stare at Ronan's perfect body. But in truth, she needed to tell him before they disrobed.

"Do you get out often?" he asked.

"Not as much as I'd like. I work too much."

He smiled. "Tell me about it."

They did have a lot in common. Did that mean they were meant for each other? As much as Blair wanted to believe Ronan was her mate, she didn't trust herself. She wanted her bear to help her, dammit.

As they neared the lake, Ronan grabbed her hand. "I want to look at the lake first. I've only been here once before, and that was in the evening."

She loved the feel of his strong grasp. His calloused palms spoke of strength and confidence. Ever since her bad experience with Jared, she'd kept her distance from men, but with Ronan, it seemed so right.

"I haven't been back much either."

Ronan faced her. "Why's that?"

"As I said, I've been busy." *Tell him.*

"But that's not the real reason, is it?"

Was she emitting a color that said she wasn't telling the whole truth? Damn. "Not entirely."

He led her over to a large log and eased her down. "Tell me. We're all alone. No one will know, and I'm good at keeping secrets."

How did he know she was harboring a secret? Had Ainsley hinted at something? Did it matter?

Or does it mean he's my mate.

Yes, yes, said a voice she hadn't heard in a long while.

Is that really you? she asked, working hard to keep the smile from her face.

Where am I? her bear asked.

Thrilled that her bear was back, albeit a little sleepy, Blair took it as a sign that Ronan was fated for her. Hadn't her bear just confirmed it? It was time to come clean.

"I dated a man by the name of Jared Henderson. Without getting into a lot of detail, he convinced me I was his mate."

Ronan stiffened. "That's not possible."

She failed to keep the smile off her face. So, Ronan knew the two of them belonged together. "I know, but he was a very persuasive man."

"How did you figure out he wasn't your mate?" Ronan asked with a knife sharp edge to his tone.

"After I learned that he was really married and that he was living a double life." His jaw tightened, and Ronan's eyes darkened. She continued. "I was in my senior year in college and saw Jared two, sometimes, three evenings a week. The rest of the time, he said he needed to travel."

"You were young and sheltered. I can see how you might have been fooled."

She wasn't that young. She should have known better. Blair clasped his hand, and a few blue sparks shot off his arm. Confident that he was her mate, she wanted to confide everything to him. "I'd like to think that's true."

Ronan's eyes turned blacker than the lake water. "If I meet the man, I'll be happy to skin him alive for you. What kind of shifter is he?"

"A bear."

The black anger seemed to disappear. "On second thought…"

She loved his flash of humor. "I bet even your wolf could take down Jared. The man was a coward."

"Did you parents freak out when they found out?"

She waited for her bear to tell her what to say, but she kept quiet. "They don't know."

His brows pinched. "If this had happened to Lexi, she would never have confided in our dad, but your parents seem wonderful."

"They are, and that's the problem. When you grow up a Murdoch, you're expected to be perfect."

Ronan rubbed her arm. "I bet it only seems that way to you. I swear Jackson breaks some law daily."

She'd never asked, but since it was for the company their father helped start, Dad probably forgave him. "I'm the only girl in the family, and I think they had higher standards for me."

"In what way?"

While Blair had spoken about this with Ainsley, it was harder telling Ronan. However, if they were to be together, there could be no secrets. "I had to dress more conservatively, act appropriately, and never lie. The usual things."

He chuckled. "Not the way I was raised. My mom was a good person, but my dad? I learned that it was okay to drink on the job and not follow directions, because it was always someone else's fault."

This time Blair grabbed his hand and squeezed. "I'm sorry. That must have been tough."

He glanced away. "It made me more resilient. In a way, he was a good role model. He taught me what not to do."

She smiled. "Way to put a positive spin on things."

"Back to you, miss perfect! What did you do after you found out that the man of your dreams was a cad?"

She would have used a stronger word for it, but she decided not to get into name calling. "I did the usual. I cried. Called him a few names, and then told him I never wanted to see him again. I was devastated and embarrassed. I felt betrayed. My bear had warned me that Jared was using me, but I wouldn't listen."

"I would never lie to you," Ronan said.

He was a sweet man. "I know."

"Anyway, I tried to put it behind me and concentrate on school." Blair inhaled, hoping she was doing the right thing in telling him the rest. "But that wasn't the worst of it. We'd been apart about a week when I found out that I was pregnant with his child." She held her breath, waiting for the censure.

Ronan didn't move. Didn't blink. Nothing. It was almost as if he'd turned to stone. Finally, he exhaled. "And the baby?"

If only Blair could read his mind to see whether he would understand or not. "I miscarried. I think it was the stress. I'd never been so distraught in my life. Not only did I fail to see what kind of man Jared was, I failed at having a baby." Blair looked upward, trying to keep the tears from falling.

"Did you really want that jerk's child?" Ronan's voice came out soft, soothing, and full of pain.

"I don't know. I told myself it was for the best that I lost the child since I wasn't ready to care for a baby, but part of me yearned for one. I would have loved him or her, but being a single mother wouldn't have been easy for either of us." The tears finally fell. "Can you see why I never told my parents?"

"From what I've seen of them, they'd understand."

Blair looked off to the side. "Maybe, but there would always be pain and disappointment—in me for being so stupid. I wasn't ready to handle it."

"Is that why you live on the other side of town?" She nodded. "You know it's best to clear the air. Misunderstandings always end badly."

"I know."

"How long has it been? Three or four years?"

He made it sound bad. "Yes. I keep saying I'm going to tell them, but the words won't come. You see, after I lost the baby, my bear went into hibernation."

"Hibernation? I've never heard of that."

She hadn't either. "I never told anyone other than Ainsley. Even she doesn't know much of it either."

"Have you been able to shift?" he asked, his voice carrying a hint of horror.

She shook her head. "I've tried, but she refuses to surface. It's as if she's blaming me for not listening to her about Jared. And I can't blame her."

Ronan lifted the hair off her shoulder. "Listen, we didn't come out here to dredge up bad memories. I shouldn't have asked why you'd distanced yourself from this beautiful place."

"You needed to know why I've been keeping to myself."

His eyes widened. "I figured being accused of murder would put a damper on anyone's spirit."

He was a nice man. "Thank you."

I want to see him naked, her bear said, sounding like her old self, and Blair smiled.

"What is it? Did you remember something?" Ronan asked.

"I didn't want to get my hopes up in case I was wrong, but I'm pretty sure my bear has been rousing since you came to my office and told me I was cleared of the murder charge."

Chapter Twelve

RONAN'S EMOTIONS WERE all over the place. Hearing about what that asshole did to Blair made him want to drive to Atlanta and confront the bastard, but knowing that her bear awoke after three years gave him hope that she might believe they were fated to be together.

He inhaled and then smiled. "I actually can tell. Your bear just added gold to your scent. I like it."

"You can tell she's awake?"

"I can sense a difference. I can feel your bear teasing my wolf now, and I like it."

Blair wiped the tears from her cheeks. "You have no idea how relieved I am to hear that."

"So has your bear forgiven you?"

"I haven't asked, and I'm not sure I want to know." Her cheer dampened. Way to go Ronan.

As much as Blair acted as if it was all in the past, it never would be until she had that talk with her family. As far as he was concerned, telling her two brothers would be the hardest conversation she'd ever have. Being highly protective, they both would want to see Jared dead, and if it weren't against the law, they might go after him.

It was the loss of the baby that stirred something deep inside Ronan. Growing up, he'd made so many promises to himself about what kind of dad he'd be. Barring something unexpected happening, he'd always be employed, come home sober, play with his kids, and always make sure they knew they were loved beyond a shadow of a doubt.

Now that he wasn't traipsing around the country and sitting in a car waiting for his bounty, he could settle down—with Blair.

Her aura has some darker reds mixed in with the pink. It's a sure sign her bear wants you.

Ronan stood and held out his hand. Blair placed her palm in his and stood. "If your bear has returned, do you want to try to shift?" She inhaled, and the colors of doubt surfaced. "It's okay if you don't succeed the first time. Your bear might need to wake up fully for a shift."

She stroked his face, and his wolf rejoiced. "When I first met you, I was highly attracted to you, but I didn't trust myself."

"You had a good reason not to. The last man treated you wrong, but what about now?"

She smiled. "I'd like to try."

Hell yes! His wolfed growled.

"Sounds good."

"How about we put our clothes on those rocks behind that tree?" Blair asked, suddenly avoiding eye contact.

Was she shy? Most shifters didn't think twice about nudity, but if she hadn't shifted in years, he could understand she might be.

"Works for me." Wanting to let her know everything would be okay, he grabbed her hand and led her over to a more secluded area.

Blair undid the top button of her shirt then twisted to the side as she slipped the material down her shoulders. Not seemingly in a rush, she folded her blouse and placed it on the rock. Was she having second thoughts? As much as he wanted to tell her she had nothing to worry about, for once he kept his opinion to himself.

When Blair reached behind her back to unhook her bra, Ronan's wolf began to pant and howl. "Let me," Ronan said as he swatted away her hands.

When she stiffened slightly, Ronan's heart squeezed. He wished he knew what to say to make things easier between them. Instead of using words—which were not his forte—he leaned over, pressed his face against her hair, and inhaled, praying she wouldn't pull away. They were mates—or would be soon—and he needed to convince her and her bear how wonderful it could be.

His fingers stopped undoing the clasp for a moment as he let the colors swirl in front of him. Pretty colors. Pinks, purples, and a hint of lime green—her favorite. Dare he believe she was turned on as much as he was?

Just as soon as he unhooked her bra, Blair twisted toward him, and his wolf demanded they shift. *Wait a little bit longer*, Ronan begged.

"Ronan?"

Their breaths mingled, and his hands traveled to her shoulders to pull down the straps. Wanting her so badly, his mind fuzzed. "Yes?"

"It's really true, isn't it?" she asked.

He didn't want to presume anything. "Do I think what is true?"

"That we are mates?"

His mouth suddenly turned dry, forcing him to swallow. "I know we are."

The smile that followed was like the sun peeking out from a dark cloud.

As much as he wanted to strip her naked and take her right there, he had to be careful. While Blair no longer faced a murder charge, the incident most likely still shook her. And then to have her bear wake up had to confuse her even more. Dare he hope it was because her bear wanted them to be together?

Yes, yes, his wolf chuffed.

Ronan finished lowering the bra straps and then placed it on top of her shirt. Holy goddess. She had the most perfect breasts he'd ever seen. Her nipples were meant to be licked, caressed, and stroked. At that thought, a sea of blue sparks shot off his body, and she giggled.

"I keep forgetting you are Wendayan," she said, her eyes wide with wonder.

"Part Wendayan, though I think of myself as mostly wolf." He stood up taller.

She leaned in closer. It was as if she'd finally made the big leap to trust him. "I like wolves. They're fast, sleek, and powerful."

"I can show you powerful right now if you like?" He'd let her decide if he was talking about their possible run or about what he really wanted—to make love to her, thrusting into her with abandon.

When she looked up at him, his vision turned nearly white from all the colors blending together—heady, heavenly, and full of happiness. This was where he needed to be. His gaze zeroed in on her lips, and he couldn't help but kiss her. Blair wrapped her arms around his neck and moaned. His bones cracked, and his blue sparks went crazy. After kicking off his boots and unzipping his pants, she acted as if she had no idea he was desperately trying to undress, because she kept kissing him, swiping her tongue around in an intricate dance that caused fire to burn deep within him.

He couldn't take it any longer and broke contact. Keeping his focus on Blair, he stepped out of his pants and discarded his briefs.

She grinned when she spotted his cock—a cock that wanted her worse than anything. "Let me finish undressing you," she said.

She could have asked him to eat dirt and he would have obliged. "Okay."

Being with his mate like this was an unimaginable experience. Two people, fated to be with each other, were about to forge a bond so close and so intense it defied description. Except for when he was young, Ronan had never known such a sense of belonging.

Blair slipped her hands under his shirt and agonizingly slowly dragged her palms up his chest, burning a path of seduction. *Hurry*, he urged, but she clearly wasn't interested in speeding through the foreplay. She seemed determined to torment him. When her hands reached his shoulders, the shirt had barely moved. Needing to help, he lifted the hem and slipped the T-shirt over his head.

Blair stepped back and ran her gaze up and down his body. "Oh, my. What big—" He smiled and ran his tongue along his canines that had sharpened. "Teeth you have." Blair laughed and Ronan chuckled.

"All the better to eat you with, my dear." He wiggled his eyebrows and winked.

Blair laughed again, and her joy altered something inside him. He sensed his mate hadn't let go of her emotions in a very long time.

"I see I'm overdressed," she said.

"Would you like my help?"

She shook her head as she unbuttoned her blue pants and kicked off her shoes. Ronan's eyes must have widened as he drank in her beauty. Her long, sun-kissed auburn hair cascaded over her shoulders, the tips kissing her breasts. And her hips were so lush and full.

"You're drooling, Ronan," she said with exceptional glee in her voice.

"I can't help it." He grabbed his cock and stroked it.

"Hey, that's my job."

Ronan glanced upward, wondering what he'd done to deserve her. "Do you think anyone will stop by? It's not exactly a private spot."

"Only a shifter would be here. When he hears your moans and groans, he'll know better than to interrupt."

He smiled. "And you, my little bear, will be silent? Don't you think I can make you scream so loud every bird will be beating a path out of here?"

She dropped back her head and laughed once more. While sounds didn't become colors, if they did, her laugh would be diamond white—pure and perfect.

"I guess we'll have to test your theory. Hop onto the rock and spread your legs for me," she said.

Normally, he took control, but for Blair, he'd oblige.

Don't you dare go off prematurely, you hear? Ronan didn't trust his wolf around her.

It's been so long, his wolf whined. *Her scent is making it extremely hard. Such pretty colors.*

He had to agree. *Try.*

Ronan jumped onto the cold rock and gave her access to his cock. As if she was born a bewitching siren, she leaned over and dragged her tongue from his balls to the tip. Her breath curled around his cock, and he emitted so many blue sparks that he practically glowed. He'd never seen anything like it before.

She looked up. "That's really cool."

Ronan was pleased her experience with Wendayans seemed to be limited. "You have a lot of colors swirling around you, too. They are so beautiful. I wish you could see them."

"Me too."

As if she couldn't wait to get back to driving him crazy, she grabbed his cock and pumped her fist. What a different experience it was compared to when he'd been in charge. Ronan had to inhale to keep from exploding though. Closing his eyes, he let the heat, the excitement, and the passion bathe him in wonder. His sparks snapped as they flew off his body.

When she drew his dick deep into her mouth, he grabbed a handful of hair and tugged. Just as she predicted, his groans rent the air. But then she did the unthinkable. Blair cupped his balls and squeezed. It was too much. Not able to stop his climax, he exploded in her mouth.

Embarrassed at the loss of control, he tried to pull back, but Blair drank him in. While it seemed impossible after being with her for a short time, his love bloomed.

When his cock finally stopped pulsating, she withdrew. Blair looked up and smiled, and his heart became hers.

"I guess you liked that," she said.

"Liked it? I loved it. It was amazing, but now it's your turn." His cock was still as hard as the rock he was sitting on, but he had to taste her—taste his mate. Ronan jumped to the ground. "Time to finish getting you undressed."

Her unbuttoned pants were easy to remove, but he left the black lacy panties on. His wolf wanted him to rip them off and sink into her right away, but she deserved more. Running a thumb along the top, he inhaled her scent.

"I thought you said something about returning the favor," Blair said, sounding more flirtatious than ever before.

"I want to savor this moment and enjoy the splash of colors radiating off your body."

Her eyes widened. "I never pictured you as a romantic."

He chuckled. "I'm not usually, but around you, I become a different person."

She stroked his chest. "I like both sides of you."

"I'm glad." Ronan knelt down in front of her, and then hooked his thumbs in her panties, willing his wolf not to rush.

Her sexual perfume was wreaking havoc with his vision though. So many colors—all so tantalizing. Ronan did a slow reveal, forcing himself not to take her too quickly. When her mahogany curls popped out, he had to beg his wolf not to sharpen his nails.

Hurry, his animal begged.

Ronan couldn't wait any longer. He tugged off her panties, and as soon as she stepped out of them, Ronan leaned over for the feast. Warmth, light, and something amazingly wonderful filled him, and he never wanted to leave her side.

WHEN RONAN OPENED her folds and swiped his tongue across her opening, Blair had never been more excited in her life. She might not be a Wendayan, but something seemed to be shooting off her body—or else it was his sparks kissing her skin. Her bear had certainly woken up!

And his kisses? A man with a beard added a lot to the experience. She loved the roughness and the sensual feel of the bristles. Now those same bristles were tickling her inner thighs. With all the licks and touches, Blair wouldn't be able to last much longer.

Needing to touch more of him, she ran her hands over his head, the texture softer than she'd expected. When Ronan slipped two fingers into her and curled them, she lifted onto her toes.

"I'm so close," she panted.

Blair had never lost control, but with Ronan, she couldn't help herself. It was almost as if he were some god who'd come to this realm to tease and delight her beyond reason. Waves of pure bliss skittered across her body. The moment he sucked on her clit, she lost it. Her body shook as her climax took hold. Her breath caught, and the near scream that escaped must have caught the attention of half the animals in Silver Lake.

Ronan leaned back on his haunches. "Beautiful," he said. With their gazes locked, Ronan stood. "I can't wait any longer. I have to have you, Blair."

He drew her close, their naked bodies pressing hard against each other. Every bad decision she'd ever made seemed to disappear. With her bear cheering her on, the kiss that followed made her lightheaded. It was as if all of her memories of anyone but Ronan were being erased. As the hair on his chest grew stiffer and fuller, her nipples tingled.

Ronan broke the contact. "I want to kiss you for hours, but my wolf and I need to be inside you."

Before she could respond, he lifted her up by her rear, allowing her to wrap her legs about his waist. With a free hand, he grabbed his shirt and spread it on the rock behind him. He then lightly pressed against the soft fabric.

"Yes," she whispered.

This seduction was surreal. Blair had never made love outside like this, but being with Ronan seemed so right.

With her arms around his neck, she delved into the heat of his mouth. His moans made all of her thoughts flee. When Ronan placed his cock at her entrance, her anticipation soared. His nostrils flared as if he was drinking in her scent and mixing it with his own. The moment her bear awoke, convincing her they were mates, she threw away all objections as to why they shouldn't be together. Now Blair wanted him more than life itself.

She dropped down on his cock and despite being slicker than rain on glass, he was too big.

"It's okay," he said, clearly understanding her dilemma. "Just relax."

Ronan dragged his lips up her neck and shivers of delight followed in its path. Every one of his touches set her body on fire, and she couldn't get enough. Blair must have diverted her attention to the wonderful sensations on her neck, because when he pulled out and entered again, he slid in farther, sending a torrent of ecstasy sizzling through her.

"That feels so fucking good," she said.

Ronan smiled. "You should be me," he whispered as he held on tight and sucked on the shell of her ear.

As if every creature in the forest was witnessing this monumental union, the birds began to chirp and animals raced to and fro. Joy speared her. Then Ronan twisted his head, and with his face close, she tasted him again. The moment their lips touched, he drove into her once more, taking her closer to that glorious climax. Their lips seemed to meld together with that drugging kiss, and her own feral desires took over. Blair pressed her feet against his thighs in order to join in the frenzied coupling.

Colors brightened, and the world seemed to stop. The air seemed crisper. Cleaner. Bolder. More alive. Holding onto him, their bodies met then retreated. Like her need for water and air, she had to have Ronan, completely and forever.

As if some magic hand was whipping them into a frenzy of desire, they fucked hard, and they fucked fast.

When he broke the kiss and dragged his lips to her neck, her climax claimed her so hard, she couldn't breathe.

"Ro-nan!"

His orgasm followed a second later. Cocooned in each other's arms, she buried her face against his shoulder, feeling more secure than she ever had in her life. He ran his hands up and down her back, soothing her and whispering how wonderful it had been. If she'd had more energy, she would have found the words to tell him the same thing. Nothing had felt so right. Ronan was her mate.

We finally found him, her bear said, sounding so content.

Blair wasn't sure whether her legs lowered to the ground or Ronan pulled out, but soon she was standing.

"You up for a dip?" he asked.

"Totally."

"Maybe your bear will want to go for a run afterward."

"Wouldn't that be nice."

Ronan grabbed her hand, and together they ran to the water. Without stopping, he charged into the lake, and Blair had no choice but to follow. Even though she enjoyed the cold, the chilly water shocked her. "Brr."

"Come here, and let me warm you up," he said.

Blair moved toward him and plastered her chest against his. Ah. Ronan's heat soaked into her, and soon she was feeling no chill at all. "That's nice."

"I'll show you nice." Ronan kissed her, and all of the heat and passion from before lit her up. "Want to race?"

She laughed. "Why would I want to do that?"

"To burn off all that excess energy you have." He nodded to her nails.

Blair lifted her chin. "You don't think you'll win, do you?"

He grinned. "Hell, yeah I do. I'll even give you a head start."

Being competitive, she took off toward the middle of the lake, but a few seconds later, Ronan grabbed her leg, drew her near, and tickled her.

Out of breath, she treaded water. "That's not fair."

"Okay, I'll swim and see if you can catch me. Anything's game." He turned around, raised one arm, and kicked.

In what seemed like seconds, he'd already reached the middle of the lake. While she tried to beat him, she failed. He was treading water and grinning when she met up with him. "Were you on the swim team or something?" she asked.

"Nope, just fast." He drew her close and kissed her again.

For the first time in years, her canines extended. Her bear was finally coming out of hibernation. As much as she wanted a repeat performance of what happened against the rock, she didn't want to deny her bear any longer and broke the delicious kiss.

She waved her hand. "I think my bear wants to show off to you."

Ronan grinned. "Is that so? Then let's go." After they swam to shore, he helped her out of the lake. "You shift first," he said. "I want to watch."

Blair inhaled and willed her animal's release. For some reason, her bear wouldn't obey. "I don't know what's wrong."

Ronan stepped up to her and rubbed her shoulders. "Maybe a few well-placed kisses will draw her out."

She loved how willing Ronan was to help. "Definitely."

The wind caressed her skin, causing goose bumps to form. A second later, she was in Ronan's arms, and he was kissing her all over. Thoughts of her making her bear appear disappeared. Just when she decided that making love again would be the best thing ever, her bones cracked, and her claws extended.

Ronan jumped back. "You can do it."

A second later, Blair was in her bear form. Wow! She wanted to shout that she'd done it, but what came out was a joyous roar. Blair kicked a rock and took off.

Ronan stood there with his arms crossed over his chest, grinning. He better shift before she was out of sight. A few seconds later, Ronan was racing next to her. Life couldn't get any better.

Chapter Thirteen

AFTER THE AMAZING love making session yesterday, followed by the plunge in the lake and the joyous run, it was time to take care of business. Ronan had to tell Lexi about their dad. To say he wasn't looking forward to this conversation was an understatement, but she'd find out soon enough—someone would talk.

He found her at her desk, entering data into a spreadsheet. Thankfully, no one was in the office waiting area.

"We need to talk," Ronan said.

Lexi leaned back in her chair. "You look different."

Wanting to please his mate, he'd trimmed his scruffy beard. "How so?"

"You look happy, but at the same time sad," Lexi said. "I guess I've lost my touch at figuring you out. We used to be so close."

That hurt. They had been close, and he was determined to make them best friends again. He pulled up a chair and faced her. "I'll start with the good news. Blair and I are mates."

Ronan hadn't expected the squeal of delight, but the hug that followed helped heal a lot of hurt.

"I'm so happy for you. So, have you two, you know?" She winked.

Hopefully, she wasn't asking if they'd officially mated, but rather if they'd made love and acknowledged they belonged together. Not a conversation he really wanted to have with his sister, so he gave her a quick simple answer. "Yes."

"I can't wait to see Blair." Lexi looked around. "Speaking of which, why aren't you with her? Is Jackson watching her?"

"Jackson didn't tell you?"

"That you caught the killer? Yes, but he said something about her not being out of the woods yet."

This conversation was going to be so hard, but hopefully Lexi wouldn't be upset that he hadn't told her right away. By the time he'd arrived home after being with Blair last night, it was late. "You know that Blair has no memory of what happened, right?"

"Yes."

"I found out why. Apparently, one of Vinea's nemeses, a goddess by the name of Darinda, came to Silver Lake a short while ago. We can't be sure, but we speculate she wanted to get back at Vinea by hurting those she loves."

Lexi scrunched up her face. "I'm confused."

"Let me start at the beginning. Dad was lured to Silver Lake by this goddess and—"

"What? Bill's here?"

"Yes. Give me a chance to explain." Not surprisingly, Lexi was a tad angry at being kept out of the loop. Her aura colors changed so quickly, he had to blink to make sure he understood everything she was feeling.

For the next fifteen minutes, he described how this woman, or rather this goddess, had duped their father into helping her, and then how he'd watch Darinda shoot Timothy Delahart. "Dad put the gun in Blair's hand and shot the weapon. I think he might have been under her spell too."

"This is unbelievable. I thought I'd never have to see him again."

"You don't have to if you don't want to." Ronan explained about their father going to Blair's house to retrieve the drugs he stole from Darinda and how Ronan's memory had been erased.

"That must have been frightening to see Bill and then not re-member anything."

"I was scared shitless to say the least."

"What did he say?" Lexi asked.

"He explained about why he denied being involved at first, and then the subsequent confession, including the fact he has cancer."

"Cancer?"

Ronan wasn't surprised to see her sympathy rise. "I'm afraid so. He asked to see you, but I told him I wasn't sure if you wanted to."

"You're right. I'm not sure."

"You have time to decide. Just let me know, and I'll take you over."

His sister looked up and smiled. "Thank you. It sounds as if Darinda is still around though and wants to cause as much havoc as possible."

"That's my guess. She might try to harm Blair because she is a Murdoch."

"Well, shit."

"My thoughts exactly."

"What are you going to do?" Lexi asked.

"When I figure it out, I'll let you know. Right now, I need to do a little digging." He leaned over and kissed his sister on the cheek. "We'll get through this."

She smiled, but the joy didn't reach her eyes. "I know we will."

Ronan headed back to his office. He had something he needed to check out first before he turned his attention to figuring out how to fight a goddess. Ever since yesterday, he couldn't banish Jared Henderson from his mind. The ass had deceived and hurt Blair. If he had been able to trust his wolf not to go haywire, Ronan would have driven down to Atlanta and had a *talk* with the dickhead. Knowing that wasn't going to happen anytime soon, Ronan still needed to learn if the man had any further interest in Blair. It didn't matter that three years had passed and that Jared hadn't tried to contact her in that time.

Ronan booted up his computer to do a search. He would have asked Jackson to perform his computer magic, but that would involve telling him Blair's secret, and he wouldn't do that to her.

Curious if Henderson's wife had ever found out about his infidelity, he looked up his name. After a short search in social media, he learned Jared Henderson was now divorced.

I'm glad the fucker got what he deserved, his wolf said.

I couldn't agree more.

Henderson had posted a few pictures of his kids and then went on to say he had one day a week visiting rights. Ronan couldn't be more pleased. A later post had a Go-Fund me request. Apparently, after his wife left him, his job suffered, and he was fired. Now he was living in an unheated trailer.

"What goes around comes around," Ronan announced.

Happy with what he'd found, he went in search of Connor to see what he could tell him about Zane Barons, the man who might be able to help him fight a demon.

"DO YOU THINK I should call Ronan?" Blair asked Ainsley.

The two of them were sitting in the break room at work. Because another therapist was in there, they kept their voices low.

"Why not? This is the twenty-first century. The man doesn't always have to make the move."

"I know, but I thought he'd call. After all, we made history together yesterday. Or at least that was what it felt like to me."

Ainsley shook her head. "You have nothing to worry about. You both admitted you were mates."

Blair smiled. "I know, and after we made love, we went for a swim in the lake." She chuckled at the remembrance. "The man was such a tease. He would tickle me and then swim to the middle of the lake where he would dare me to follow."

Ainsley grinned. "Which you did."

"Of course. I'm telling you the man can kiss."

"So, what's the problem? Clearly, you belong together. I'm betting Ronan is trying to give you a little space. His wolf is probably going crazy right now. I know Jackson and I were like that." Her eyes widened. "Sorry. Too much information. No one likes to hear about their siblings having sex."

She laughed. "You're right. Ronan is considerate like that, but I miss him."

"That's a good thing, but be aware once you mate, it will be worse for a while."

"I've heard that, but I doubt my need can become more intense."

"Just you wait." Her friend rubbed her arm. "I can't tell you how happy I am for you. You glow."

"This feels so right." Blair wasn't so naïve to think all was right in the world. Darinda was out there, and there was no telling what crap she was planning. Blair checked her watch, then pushed back her chair and stood. "I have a patient in a few minutes."

"Are you seeing Ronan tonight?"

"Yes."

Ainsley grinned. "I bet I can guess what you two will be doing."

Heat raced up her face. "We'll see."

RONAN CALLED BLAIR to let her know he had some work to handle, but that he'd stop over once he was free. "I asked Jackson to look in on you until I get there."

"What do you have to do that's so important?" she asked.

Because he wished to delay her worry for as long as possible, he decided not to give her any details. "Just something for work. Don't worry. I'll be as quick as possible."

"I miss you."

He grinned. His wolf was already acting up. "You'll have to show me how much."

"Oh, I plan to."

Once he disconnected, he went to work on watching videos on how to fight with a two-handed sword—specifically with a Katana, which was one of the sharpest of the swords—as well as with a broad sword, trying to figure out which would work best on a goddess. It was amazing what one could learn from the Internet.

At six, he headed over to Zane and Missy's place, hoping Zane could help in some way, even though over the phone, he didn't sound all that confident. Ronan knocked and a giant of a man answered. Sure, Connor had mentioned Zane was big, but Ronan didn't expect someone so huge. No wonder he'd been able to defeat a demon.

"You must be Ronan. Come in," Zane said with a smile.

A pretty woman who was holding a baby came forward. She held out her hand. "Hi, I'm Missy."

Her colors were soft—sea foam green and pale grays with a splash of intermittent whites. Zane's were different. His colors were ones Ronan had a hard time defining, but the overall tone was orange.

"Nice to meet you both."

"Come in," Zane said. "Tell me about this goddess and why you want to fight her."

"I don't want to fight her, but she's already stolen my memory and the memory of my mate."

"Mate?" Missy asked.

Whoops. Maybe he should have asked Blair if she minded if he told people. "Blair Murdoch."

Missy's colors heightened as she smiled brightly. "I'm so happy for you two. Can I get you a beer?"

"I'm good. I can't stay long."

Zane led him over to the sofa. "Tell me what you know about this goddess."

"That's one of the problems. I don't know much. Vinea told us that Darinda can erase memories, but she didn't say much else, other than the only way to kill her was to cut off her head."

"Hmm. I must confess I'm skeptical. On Cargonia, it's almost impossible to kill a demon, and they aren't even immortal. I got lucky and caught one off guard."

"I see." This wasn't looking good.

"But I understand your concern. You must protect your mate at all costs. I can make you a sword of the finest steel. I've read up on your swords of the fifteenth century, and while there are many, none are quite like mine. I make mine with some special powers infused in the steel that can prove very useful." He held up a hand. "But unless you know how to use it, I doubt you can get the drop on a goddess."

"I have to try."

Zane nodded. "I understand. It will take me a few days to find the right steel and then another few days to forge the blade. In the meantime, I can show you how to fight." He smiled. "We'll use sticks. I don't want to accidentally kill you."

Ronan enjoyed his sense of humor. "Blair might come after you if you do." Or least he hoped she'd be upset enough to want some revenge. "Speaking of which, I need to get back to her. Let me know when you have time to give me some lessons. In the meantime, I'll try to learn something on my own."

Both men stood. After he thanked Zane profusely, he rushed off, needing to see Blair.

Chapter Fourteen

A S SOON AS Ronan jumped in his Jeep, he called his mate.
"Hey. Where are you?" She sounded excited instead of upset, which pleased him to no end.

"I just finished up with something. Have you eaten?" Asking a question after the statement would temporarily keep her from wanting to know more details.

"Not yet."

"Perfect. What do you say I pick up something to eat and bring it over?" Hopefully, Blair would be the dessert.

I love it, his wolf panted.

"That would be wonderful."

"See you soon." Ronan probably should have asked what she was in the mood for, but she'd mentioned that one of her favorite foods was Chinese. While he hadn't been to Wong's before, Zane had recommended it. Seemed the big bear loved food he couldn't get on Cargonia.

Once Ronan placed the order and they filled it, he took off, anxious to be with Blair. When he arrived at her house, her car sat in the same spot as when his father had tried to take the drugs he'd hidden. Jackson was parked next to her.

Even though a goddess had duped his dad, he wouldn't have ended up in jail if he'd been able to overcome his addiction in the first place. Ronan did have some sympathy for the old man. Losing one's mate had to be hard, but gambling wasn't the answer.

As soon as Blair answered the door, her scent overwhelmed him. The colors of the warm summer night blended with hers, making it hard to remember to say hello.

She smiled, and his wolf told him to skip dinner and go straight to dessert.

Settle down. We'll enjoy her soon enough, he told his overly excited animal. *We don't want her to think we are only here for sex, you idiot. A woman like Blair needs to be shown how much we appreciate her.*

For once, his wolf kept quiet, and Ronan was able to exhale.

Blair had changed out of her work clothes. Now she was barefoot, wearing short shorts, and a green top that would be easy to remove. *Stop it.* He'd come here to talk with her. Though making love would come later if things went well.

"It smells wonderful," she said, nodding to the package in his hand.

"It's Chinese." He twisted the bag to show her the logo on the front.

She sucked in a breath. "It's from Wongs!"

He stepped inside and set the package on the table then drew her close. "I've missed you," he whispered.

Jackson cleared his throat. "I need to head on back to Ainsley. Take care you two, and don't do anything I wouldn't do."

Ronan was slipping. He hadn't even noticed her brother was sitting on the sofa. "Sure thing!"

They all laughed. Once Jackson left, Ronan returned his attention to Blair. Her eyes had changed colors, as had her scent. Wrapping her arms around his neck, she leaned in for a kiss Ronan could no more deny than he could forgive his father for all his wrongdoings. Sparks flew, and his cock hardened. Even though she tasted like honey and smelled like fresh linen, he needed to discuss something with her first.

After drinking in his fill, he leaned back. "How about we eat first? I don't want my stomach grumbling during *dessert*."

Blair looked around, obviously checking for a bag from a bakery.

"Dessert?"

Ronan let his eyes roam her body from head to toe, lingering on the good parts, before raising an eyebrow to her. He could see Blair's sudden intake of breath, and then she gave him a sexy little smirk. "Ooohh my, yes! Yes, there will be many other sounds during dessert, and we wouldn't want one of them to be your stomach." She giggled.

He tipped his head back and laughed. Once the murder charge had been dropped and her bear had reemerged, she had become a different person—freer, happier, and sexier, if that was even possible.

Ronan gave Blair a light swat on the ass as she stepped into the small galley style kitchen, and she gave a little yelp. She opened the cupboard and then handed him the dishes. "How about putting your hands to a different use and setting the table?" she asked.

Ronan grinned. "Can do."

A moment later, she followed him into the postage stamp dining room, carrying the silverware and glasses filled with water.

"I was thinking," he said.

"About what?" she asked as she opened the paper bag and extracted the containers of food.

"I don't like inconveniencing anyone, and I've been at the McKinnon's guesthouse for a while now."

She looked up at him. "Are you thinking of moving?" Her colors swirled around her, but he wasn't able to get a lock on her thoughts.

Would she be receptive to him moving into her place? They hadn't known each other for long, but they were fated mates. If her body was as needy as his, she might agree.

"Yes." He waited a beat to see if she'd suggest she'd be willing for him to share her bed, but Blair said nothing.

Ask her, his wolf urged. *The worst she can say is no, but I bet she won't.*

"Seeing as how we are mates, I thought it might be a good idea to spend more time together." When her lime green swirled around the pink hues, he grew bolder. "What do you think about me moving in here? I'd split the rent, of course."

When she smiled, every ounce of anxiety drained away. "I'd love that."

"Are you sure?"

What the hell are you doing? his wolf asked. *She said yes. Just shut up.*

"I think it's a great idea, though would you fit?" She waved a hand. "The bed is only a queen, and a small one at that, and my closet is already bursting at the seams."

He looked around. "I can keep most of my things in my Jeep."

"You don't have to do that. I can store my winter clothes at my parents' house, and then swap them out for my summer stuff when the time comes."

"Or we could get a place of our own." His heart beat faster. Ronan had always dreamed of settling down, but he never dared believe he'd find his mate, especially when he traveled from town to town chasing criminals. When her colors changed, Ronan feared he'd gone too far.

"I doubt we'd find a rental in the compound where my parents live though," she said.

He slowly let out the breath he was holding. "As long as we're together, I don't care where it is."

Her grin said it all. "Me either. Now that we've cleared that up, how about telling me where you were tonight?"

Oh shit. Someone must have leaked the information. Blair did work with Ainsley who was mated to Jackson. It made sense he might have let something slip. Ronan never wanted to hide anything from Blair, but he didn't want her to worry either. When some angry colors swirled off her, he decided to come clean. "I was visiting Zane Barons."

"Zane? Why?"

"How about we eat, and I tell you about it?"

"Okay."

They scooped out their food, but from the way Blair eyed it, she'd lost her appetite. Damn. "I asked him to make me a sword and teach me how to use it."

Her hand tightened on her fork. "Because of Darinda?"

"Yes. We can't rule out that Darinda doesn't want to inflict pain on Vinea by attacking one of us."

Her brows pinched. "I don't know why she would? I don't remember anything, so I can't point a finger at her. And even if I could, what harm can it do? She'd disappear and hightail it back to the dark realm."

Ronan wasn't sure what to believe anymore. "I know, but we can't assume she'll be logical. According to Vinea, Darinda was jealous of her. It's possible, though not likely, that she'll want to show us how powerful she is."

"By killing me?"

"Or me. I work at Devon's brother's firm. That would bring pain to Vinea—or so I'm assuming—and to several who work there. It's possible Devon would have to return to Silver Lake to help out."

Blair slumped in her chair. "And I'm a Murdoch."

"Yes. I imagine Darinda knows that your father is the Associates part of McKinnon and Associates. I would suggest we leave town, but if a goddess wants to find us, there is no place on Earth to hide." Ronan could feel her pain—and see it too. "Which is why I want to be prepared."

"Prepared for what? Death?" she asked.

He set down his spoon. "I might get lucky. Zane wasn't very hopeful that anyone could kill a goddess, but he said he had a few tricks he could provide me with."

She huffed. "I don't believe this. Here I thought I was lucky when I beat the murder charge. Now we could both die."

Ronan pushed back his chair, not able to take the waves of pain rolling off her. He stood and opened his arms. "Come here."

The moment she stepped into his embrace, their bodies seemed to melt into one another, and her colors softened. Blair placed her head on his shoulder and held him tight. As much as he wanted to make slow love to her, she was hurting right now. He'd have to wait until she was ready.

She finally looked up at him. "I forgot to mention that tomorrow is my mother's birthday."

That came out of nowhere. Most likely Blair was trying not to think about their terrible circumstances. "And?"

A small smile lifted her lips. "We've been invited to a party at the McKinnon's. Vinea will be there."

His pulse rose. "I'd love to talk to her. Maybe she can give me some pointers on how to defeat Darinda. She might have a weakness that only another goddess would know about."

"Perhaps, but don't ask her to intervene. Remember, she is five months pregnant."

"I would never do such a thing."

Blair stroked his face. "I know. You're a good man." She ran a palm down his arm and clasped his hand. "How about sitting with me on the sofa where we can snuggle?"

Ronan worried about her. "You don't want to finish eating? You hardly ate anything."

"I'm not in the mood. Maybe later. I do know what would help me feel better." The pinks and purples, along with that enticing lime green swirled around her as she looked up at him and smiled.

He could guess. "And what's that?"

"Why don't I show you?"

"Now you're talkin'."

AFTER LEARNING THAT she and Ronan might be targeted by someone as powerful as a goddess, Blair wanted to cry and yell and beat something, but she was smart enough to know it wouldn't do any good. If they did only have a short time on Earth, she wanted to enjoy being with Ronan as much as possible.

Just learning that he wanted to move in with her convinced her they would find love in each other's arms. Ronan led her over to the sofa, and just as he was about to sit down, she stopped him.

"I think a few well-placed kisses would help me deal from the shock of learning that we don't have as much control over our lives as we'd hoped," she said.

Ronan flipped an errant strand of hair behind her ear, sending her pulse soaring.

Take off his clothes and fuck him hard, her bear shouted, the interruption startling her since she wasn't used to having her animal in her head.

Don't worry. I know what I want.

Ronan cupped her face. "I want you so bad, but if you want to wait, I'll understand."

"Not on your life."

As if someone had fired a starter's pistol, they tore at each other's clothing. Trapped between the sofa and the coffee table, they moved to the end of the sofa where Ronan had her naked in seconds, but only because she wasn't wearing much. He'd managed to kick off his shoes while she struggled to lower his jeans.

He stepped back. "Let me."

With his golden eyes focused on her, he ditched the rest of his clothes in seconds. Next thing she knew, their bodies were plastered against each other, his chest hair tickling her nipples. The kiss that followed had her own bones cracking. Ronan turned his head, causing his beard to caress her lips and chin. This time, she was the one to step back since her needs became so great.

"I want you now," she said.

His gaze traveled over her body. "Your colors are exquisite. Pure. Alive. Sensual."

"I'm happy and excited."

"I love it." Ronan inhaled. When he closed his eyes, the lines on his forehead almost disappeared.

Blair smiled, and then ran her hands down his corded back. His muscles bunched and flexed, almost as if he was showing off.

"Kiss me again," she demanded.

Ronan's eyes opened. Not only did the kiss curl her toes, waves of excitement thrummed her sex. With his hard length pressed against her, she was no longer able to resist. Because the bedroom seemed a mile away, Blair broke the kiss, turned around, and grabbed the sofa arm. When she widened her legs, Ronan groaned and stepped behind her. "You're determined to make me shift, aren't you?"

That was the last thing she wanted. "No, I need you too much."

When Ronan placed his hard cock at her entrance and palmed her tits, she thought she might be the one to prematurely explode this time. His fingers twirled the tips as he kissed her shoulder and then her neck. As much as she thrilled to the excitement of his touch, she needed his cock more. Once her bear had woken up, her sex drive had gone berserk. Ronan seemed to have altered something inside her.

"Please Ronan, I'm ready."

Chapter Fifteen

RONAN WORKED HARD not to drive into Blair. Her life was crumbling around her, and he didn't want to make it any harder on her, but damn, his wolf was scratching and clawing and howling for him to take her hard.

As soon as she begged him though, he eased into her, trying not to rush. Ronan wanted her to understand that she was precious to him. She was his mate, and the woman he wanted to spend the rest of his life with—no matter how long that life might last.

Blair sucked in a breath and arched her back, her mewling turning into a full-blown groan. "Yes!"

He traced his lips up to the shell of her ear, keeping away from her delicate neck. Despite his desire to mate with her right now, it was too soon.

No, it's not, his wolf shot back. *Do you want to die before you mate?*

If he listened to his damn wolf, his animal would lead him down the wrong path. Blair leaned forward, his dick sliding out part way. When she pressed back, all of his control flew out the window. Her wet slickness engulfed him again, and his halo of blue nearly encompassed her. His bones cracked, and his nails grew.

I will not shift. I will not shift. For Blair he had to keep in control.

It was when she placed her forehead on the sofa arm, changing the angle of entry that he lost it. Nothing would stop him from bringing her to climax first though. As if she was of the same mind, he drove into her just as she pumped back her hips again. His fingers pinched then caressed her nipples, causing her breaths to increase and her moans to grow louder.

"Come for me, Blair."

She lifted her head and let out a scream. "Ro-nan."

His hot seed filled her, and in his mind's eye, he could see their cubs playing in a field, happy and healthy.

Colors swam, and their slick bodies weakened. He slipped his hands to her hips and pressed his chest against her sensual back. Ronan then wrapped his arms around her, waiting for his pulse to slow. If this was what life was going to be with his mate, he damn well better win the fight against that goddess.

BLAIR HAD FOUND the perfect birthday presents for her mom. A new kitchen store had opened in Andersonville, and in it she'd found a turkey baster, some beautiful drying cloths, and a heavy gage stainless steel pot that her mom had been talking about for two years.

Ronan had suggested he drive over there with her, but she told him to spend as much time with Zane as he could. Besides, if Darinda wanted to kill her, she'd probably wait until the two of them were together before she lowered the proverbial boom.

When Blair returned from her shopping spree, Ronan had moved some of his things into her place. Even though he didn't bring much, her one-bedroom was clearly too small for the two of them. Ronan might only be a shade above six-feet, but he took up a hell of a lot space.

Soon they'd have to begin their search for a bigger place of their own. After what she'd been through with Jared, that thought should have put her in a state of panic, but it didn't. Being with Ronan was the right thing to do. While the specter of death floated above their heads, Blair refused to let it ruin what little time she might have left on Earth.

She hoped that Darinda would be called out on another assignment and forget about her need for revenge against Vinea. Right. And Blair would suddenly be endowed with a power so great that one look would make the goddess retreat to the dark realm.

Refusing to let anything ruin her mom's birthday party though, Blair stepped into the bedroom to see what was taking Ronan so long. Her bear stirred then roared at the luscious sight. Ronan was dressed in black jeans and black boots and was shirtless. No one had ever looked better to her. "You're not ready? I thought the woman was supposed to take more time."

He looked over his shoulder. "I'm nervous to meet your mom. I want her to like me." He spun to face her. "Do you like the black shirt or the white one?" He held up both.

Blair honestly didn't think it mattered, but a man always looked good in white. "The black might make you appear a little sinister. But don't worry about my mom. She'll love you no matter what you wear."

He laughed. "I hope so," he said as he slipped on the white one.

Once dressed, they piled into his Jeep. Ronan carried the presents Blair had purchased, while she carried the tin of chocolate chip cookies she'd made. She might not be a great chef, but her mom had taught her at a young age how to bake cookies.

"When are you going to tell the McKinnon's that you've moved out?" she asked.

He glanced over at her. "I spoke with Mr. McKinnon already. He said he was sad to see me go, but he understood."

Blair said little during the rest of the drive. The pep talk she needed to give herself required a lot of concentration. While she didn't know Vinea that well, everyone in both the McKinnon and Murdoch families seemed enchanted by her. Her redemption had had some bumps along the way, but she'd overcome a lot to get where she was today.

Ronan pulled down the McKinnon's driveway, past several parked cars. "Do you mind if we park at the guest cottage and walk back? I can't find a place that's any closer. I didn't expect such a crowd," he said.

"That's fine. Both of our families like to have get-togethers and invite everyone. It's been that way ever since I can remember."

He nodded. "And your parents know we're mates, right?"

She looked over at him and smiled. "Yes. I told them. They were thrilled. You have nothing to worry about. You're a family member now."

He cut the engine and then came over to her side to open the door. While Ronan acted like his usual gallant self, he still seemed tense. Most likely it was about waiting for the possible confrontation with Darinda.

As soon as Blair climbed out, she straightened her shoulders and inhaled the warm summer air. Being surrounded by loved ones would surely help erase the doom circling them.

"Why is the party at the McKinnon's instead of at your house?" Ronan asked.

"So my mom doesn't have to do anything—including clean up."

"Smart."

Once they reached the McKinnons' house, Blair opened the door and was met with laughter and loud chatter. As if Darinda told them she wasn't going to mess with them—ever—the tension in Blair's back and shoulder evaporated.

"Blair!" her mother said as she hurried toward them. While it seemed as if she was looking at her, Mom was definitely scoping out Ronan.

"Happy birthday, Mom," she said, holding the cookies away from her body.

They hugged and kissed, and then her mom leaned back. "Introduce me to your young man."

Ronan stuck out his hand. "Ronan Laramie," he said. "Nice to meet you."

Her mother's eyes widened in appreciation. "How nice to finally meet you."

"Where shall I put the cookies?" Blair asked.

"On the table. And the presents go on the coffee table in the living room, but you shouldn't have."

Her mother went through the denial thing every year. "You're only sixty once," Blair shot back.

"Ugh. Don't remind me!"

Once they deposited the gifts and goodies, Blair looked around the room. Most of the family members seemed to be there. Rye and Izzy were surrounded by a group of relatives cooing at their baby Logan, while Kalan's mate, Elana was keeping watch on their two-year old who was happy to wander about.

Ainsley came up to them and hugged Blair. "Where are the twins?" Blair asked.

"They're napping in the bedroom. I'll bring them out shortly."

"I can't wait to see them. Are Vinea and Devon here?" Blair asked.

"They haven't arrived. I think she called EmmaLee about half an hour ago and said they were running a little late."

As if the goddess was waiting to make a grand entrance, she and Devon McKinnon knocked, and then stepped inside. Blair nudged Ronan. "That's Devon and Vinea."

After the McKinnons had greeted their son and his mate, Blair and Ronan approached the couple.

"I need to introduce myself," Ronan said. He and Blair strode up to Devon and shook his hand. He then turned to Devon's mate. "I'm Ronan. Lexi's brother."

She smiled. "Ah, yes. I've heard good things about you." She faced Blair. "I'm so sorry about what happened," Vinea said. "Has Darinda made an appearance?"

"Only to my father in jail," Ronan said, answering for her.

Blair bet Vinea was tired after her long journey. For being five months pregnant, she looked wonderful. "Let's sit down. Can I get you something to drink?"

"I'd love a glass of water," Vinea said.

Most likely the goddess could conjure one up, but she'd heard Vinea was trying to fit into this world.

"I'll get it," Devon said. "You two chat."

Ronan followed him, probably to talk a bit of shop. She turned back to Vinea. "How are you feeling?"

Talking about children was a subject Blair always avoided. Even though she wanted a child, she wasn't sure she was built to bear one—no pun intended.

"It was a little rough at first, but I feel great now. You? How have you been holding up?"

"Like what you would expect." She told Vinea about how Ronan planned to learn to fight with a sword in case Darinda challenged him.

"Is he going to walk around with it dangling from his waist or something? I'm not sure that's the best idea. A sword is about the only thing that can kill Darinda, but I doubt she'll make an appearance if he's wearing one. Then again, Darinda isn't the brightest bulb in the realm. She's so freaking arrogant, she might try to call Ronan out."

Blair's determination not to become depressed just flew out the proverbial window after that comment. Before she could ask Vinea any more questions, Ronan and Devon returned. He handed Vinea her water.

Blair and Ronan sat across from Vinea and Devon. "I'm sorry to hear a dark realm goddess has you in her sight," Devon said.

"Tell me about it."

Vinea patted the seat next to her. "Come here for a minute."

Blair switched sofas and sat next to her. Vinea reached out and clasped Blair's hand then closed her eyes. While she had no idea what Vinea was up to, she trusted her.

"I can feel the remnants of evil inside you where Darinda erased your memory."

That was totally creepy. It was bad enough that part of her conscious had been altered, but to leave some evil inside her freaked her out. Who knew what a bit of evil remaining could do down the line. "Can you remove it?"

Vinea opened her eyes. "I can try."

"Vinea?" Devon said. "You don't need to be absorbing Darinda's evil."

She shook her head. "It won't be like when I heal someone. I will be putting my light into Blair, and the light will cancel the evil."

"Will I get my memory back?" Blair asked. She wasn't sure she wanted to remember the shooting, though Ronan had already detailed what had happened.

"Yes, but more importantly, Darinda won't have a hold over you anymore."

Blair looked over at Ronan who nodded. "Ronan had his memory erased, too."

"Okay, Ronan, switch places with Devon. I need to be touching both of you for this to work."

He sat on the other side of Vinea. While Blair was aware of the talking and laughing going on around her, it seemed as if they were in a cocoon surrounded by an impenetrable dome—a place where no harm could come to her. Vinea might not be immortal anymore, but she seemed to possess a lot of abilities.

Vinea grasped their hands tight. "Now close your eyes and concentrate on clearing your mind. I must have your complete attention."

Blair did as she asked. Images flitted across her mind, but she tried to keep them at bay in order for Vinea to do her job. A sharp ache stabbed her heart, and the image of an old man bending next to her car appeared. Wait a minute. That wasn't her memory. It was Ronan's. Just as she was about to say something had gone wrong, Vinea let go.

"Can you remember what happened now?" Vinea asked to no one in particular.

Blair opened her eyes to see Ronan's gaze on hers. She glanced to the side in order to concentrate. Like a tidal wave of photos, the movie unfolded from her walking out of the back door to seeing that woman hold the gun and shoot a man. "Yes," she whispered, not sure if she wanted to see what had really happened.

Blair dropped her head in her hands. A second later, Ronan moved next to her and clasped her shoulders. "It's okay. We need to use it to our advantage."

He was right. She looked up at him. "What an evil woman. She just shot Timothy Delahart without provocation."

"She is evil," Ronan said.

Blair sniffled, unable to keep her hands from shaking. "I know what Darinda looks like now, unless she changed her hair color and length."

Vinea smiled. "That's my trick, not Darinda's. I can't erase memories like she can. If I had her talent, I would have deleted all the bad things I'd previously done to Devon from his mind."

Devon smiled. "It worked out for the best. I love you more because of what you went through. Now if you're finished, how about we chat with the others?"

"I'd like that."

The love in Devon's eyes was inspiring. While Blair would have liked to pick her brain further, she understood that Vinea and Devon's time in Silver Lake was limited.

Devon helped Vinea up. Before she took a step, Ronan reached up and touched Vinea's arm. "If Darinda does decide to take us out so to speak, do you know of any weaknesses she might have that I can exploit?"

Her brows rose, and Vinea's cute smile spoke of mischief. "I know of a few things you can try."

Chapter Sixteen

FOR THE NEXT three weeks, Ronan spent every night practicing his sword wielding skills with Zane. His new good friend had made two amazing swords unlike anything he'd ever seen. While they both weighed twelve pounds, Zane handled his as if it were no more than a gun whereas Ronan still struggled with the four-foot length. However, if he wanted to cut off a person's head, he believed this would be the ticket.

Zane held his sword in front of his face. "Are you ready for another round?"

"Yes. What should I focus on today?" Ronan asked. "The footwork is getting easier for me, but my swinging technique is slow and clumsy."

"How about trying to cut off a head? I think you're ready for this next step."

Ronan laughed. "Excuse me? Not that I believe I'll succeed, but all it would take is one lucky swing, and I doubt Missy would forgive me."

Zane laughed. "I wasn't talking about my head. Missy has watermelons planted in the garden. I bet she won't mind if we borrow a few."

"That I can do."

They both walked toward the back of the property where a variety of vegetables and herbs were planted. "She's okay with decimating a few?" Ronan asked.

"Yes, if it's for a good cause."

"Vinea said that Darinda has her weaknesses, but what if she conjures up some kind of magic sword to use against me. I won't stand a chance."

"It's possible," Zane said. "You said Vinea told you that Darinda doesn't possess the skill to use a blade effectively. However, if the metal of her blade holds enough magic, there might be nothing you can do against her." Zane's cheer suddenly disappeared.

"Then why am I trying?" Ronan hated himself for sounding dejected. He had to suck it up and try. "Never mind. Let's do this."

Zane's grin returned, obviously trying to bolster Ronan's spirits. "Okay then. I think we should focus on the best angle to slice off a person's head." He picked an eight-inch diameter watermelon. "Let me demonstrate."

He placed the melon on a log. With one quick slice, the top half of the fruit rolled to the ground. "A slightly downward stroke works quite well. Given Darinda is a few inches shorter than you, you just need to swing naturally."

"Let me give it a try."

They took the fruit to the front of the house, where Ronan placed it on the hood of his Jeep. If he didn't want to ruin the finish, he needed to be accurate.

"I'm ready."

AFTER TWO HOURS of cutting watermelons, Ronan's arms had turned to rubber, but his spirits had improved, in part because Zane deemed him worthy of fighting any fruit. His friend's patience and wonderful sense of humor helped Ronan slog through the long workouts. Connor had been wonderful also, allowing him to take time off whenever Zane had a free moment. Missy deserved a lot of credit for graciously giving up her mate for hours on end.

When Ronan arrived home, all he could think of was a hot shower and some even hotter sex. All during his workout, he'd been distracted. His wolf kept turning Ronan's focus to Blair's wonderful breasts, her sassy mouth, and divine body. To say the least, his aim had gone awry. He could still hear Zane chastise him every time his eyes turned golden.

But now he didn't have a sword—at least not one made of metal. That one was safely stored in a long leather case he left in the back of his Jeep.

After unlocking the front door, he stepped inside to the heavenly scent of something cooking.

Blair came out of the kitchen and smiled as she wiped her hands on a towel. "How did it go?"

"Zane dubbed me master of the watermelon."

Her brows drew downward. "And that helps you how?"

"Let's just say, I improved my ability to aim and cut cleanly."

"Ah." She moved closer with a sensual look in her eyes, and his wolf sat up and took notice.

He held up his hands. "I'm not fit to be around."

She wrinkled her nose then laughed. "You definitely have a man-sweat odor about you."

That was an understatement. He was almost blinded by his stench. "I'm going to shower. I'd ask you to join me, but I'm not sure I have the energy to lift the soap and wash your back. Besides, you might pass out before I get clean."

"You might be right," she shot back with eyes that sparkled gold.

As he headed down the hallway, Blair's wonderful laugh followed, the colors dancing around him, lightening his step.

Once in the shower, the heat sluicing over his body helped soothe his sore muscles, but it might be days before he was back to one hundred percent. The image of Darinda kept edging its way into his head. Both Blair and Vinea had described her in such detail that he was certain he'd recognize her when he saw her, no matter if she had altered her appearance or not. Vinea said Darinda's cruel black eyes would be a giveaway.

He slapped his palm against the shower wall. It wasn't fair. He finally had everything he wanted in life, and then some vindictive dark goddess bitch decided to exact revenge on Blair—or rather on Vinea by wanting to kill Blair.

When they spoke with Vinea again at the party, she'd said that Androf would be displeased that one of his own had left witnesses. Darinda's honor was at stake to clean up her mess. Damn.

A knock sounded on the bathroom door. "You okay in there?" Blair asked.

"I'm fine." He'd been wallowing in self-pity for too long. He did a final scrub and rinse before shutting off the water and stepping out.

She knocked again and eased open the door. The steam swirled around her, encasing his beautiful mate in a mystical cloud. When her eyes widened, he completely forgot about swords, dark goddesses, and revenge.

"You clean up nicely," Blair said as she lifted her top to expose the prettiest pink bra.

As if all the fatigue had been swept away by the sight of her beauty, Ronan advanced, his gaze bouncing between her beautiful smile and those delicious tits. "That's because I'm refreshed; ready for anything."

Blair grinned. "Anything?" She grabbed his cock, a sly smile teasing her lips.

"Anything."

Colors abounded, and his energy soared. Ronan reached behind her back with one hand and unhooked her bra. Her gaze never leaving his face, Blair helped him by sliding the silky straps down her arms.

Without a word, she grabbed his hand and led him toward the bedroom. His wolf howled, and Ronan could wait no longer. He plastered her against the hallway wall and devoured her lips. His feral instincts reached a new high, and desperate for her taste, he delved into her mouth. He closed his eyes, and her lime green hues blended with the pinks and purples so vividly his libido shot into high gear, rejoicing at the onslaught of endorphins.

If their time together was going to be cut short by the dark goddess, he wanted to be with Blair as intimately and as often as possible.

Her nails scraped down his back, sending shivers of need straight through him. Not breaking the seal, he slipped her shorts and panties past her hips but his reach wasn't enough.

Blair kicked off her sandals and moved to the side. She dragged her shorts down her hips, and as she bent over to step out of them, her mouth happened to find his cock. Dear goddess. His wolf sang, and his need exploded. "That feels so fucking good," he grunted.

Unable to take any more, he tried to guide her upward, but she moaned and shook her head. Who was he to stop her from sucking on his cock?

Not me, his wolf chimed in.

Unbelievable erotic pulses shot up his hard shaft, forcing Ronan to use all of his willpower not to shift or come. Blair had a hold over him that was unlike anything he'd ever experienced.

Take her, his wolf begged. *We need her.*

I know.

Just as he was about to lose it, Blair released him and stood. Wrapping her arms around his neck, she pressed her breasts against his chest and kissed him hard. When she wiggled her hips against his dick, he broke. Ronan could no longer keep from loving her. Lifting her up by her butt, he walked them toward the bedroom, and she wrapped her legs around his waist, exciting him further.

"I've missed you today. I want you to fuck me hard, Ronan."

At her glorious words, his blue glow pulsed and expanded. He pressed his face against her cheek. "I intend to," he whispered a second before he ran his tongue along the soft spot on her neck.

She moaned, and he eased her onto the bed. As much as he wanted to lick her tiny pearl nub until she screamed her release, if he waited any longer, his wolf would make his presence known.

Kneeing open her legs, Ronan drove into her with one push. White-hot heat swamped him as a myriad of colors swam in front of his eyes, and his blue Wendayan sparks danced around her.

"Oh, Ronan." Blair's eyes opened wide as she gulped in air, arching her back. She grabbed a handful of his hair and tugged. When she let out a primitive cry, a shock of pure bliss sped through him.

As if his wolf decided he was in charge, he demanded Ronan withdraw then thrust into her again, which he happily did. Blair met him with an equal push of her own. At that moment, it was as if they were floating on the same beautifully colored wavelength, matching each other's passion.

Dropping her head back, she opened her mouth, exposing two sharpened incisors. Her golden eyes hazed over as if she were holding on by a thread.

"Let it go, Blair. Come with me."

As if she'd been waiting to hear those words, she sucked in a large breath, closed her eyes, and sent out a keening sound so deliciously decadent that Ronan could not hold back any longer.

"Yes!" Her grip tightened, and her muscles tensed.

His climax shot his hot seed into her. It seemed like minutes before his breathing slowed. Ronan rolled over and dragged Blair on top of him, wrapping his arms around her.

Her body sagged, and she patted his shoulder. "I needed that," she said.

She needed that? "I needed it more."

She mumbled something he couldn't understand, but all he cared about was holding her in his arms forever.

BLAIR PLACED THE bowl of spaghetti on the table, along with the meat sauce and garlic bread, while Ronan poured the wine. She couldn't keep the good news to herself any longer. "Guess what?"

"From the shimmery pinks radiating off you, it's good news. I could sure use some."

Blair had debated telling Patsy not to bother looking for a place for them since they might not live long enough to move in, but then she decided that kind of negative energy was not healthy. "Patsy Howard, a local realtor, thinks she's found a place for us."

They'd been looking for over a week, and nothing seemed to fit the bill.

"Really? That is good news."

Even though her one-bedroom was small, during the month that they'd lived together, they'd found a certain rhythm, allowing them to find their own space when needed. Blair had moved some of the clothes she wasn't wearing at the moment into her old room at her parents' home, providing space for most of Ronan's stuff.

Blair sat down at the table, and Ronan followed. "I know it's probably a little premature to be looking for a place since we have no idea what Darinda is planning, but frankly, I'm tired of waiting," she said. "We haven't seen or heard from her in over a month."

Ronan sipped his wine. "I've been thinking the same thing. We should remain cautiously optimistic and live each day to the fullest." He held up a finger. "But I still want to keep my sword fighting skills honed."

"I agree. Don't worry, I'll make sure not to be alone for any length of time, though how I can stop her from suddenly appearing in my office or here, I don't know."

Ronan's teeth extended, and his eyes darkened. "We can't let her get into our heads. She's probably waiting for us to let our guard down. Then she'll make her move."

"That's not a pleasant thought. It's not easy to pretend all is well though. Even my patients have begun to ask me if everything is all right. I don't like to lie, but I'm not about to say that I'm waiting for a goddess to seek revenge against me for something I haven't done."

"Panicking or losing sleep over the wait only feeds into Darinda's hand," he said.

"That is even more depressing."

Ronan leaned forward and moved an errant strand of hair behind her ear. "When can we see our potential future home?"

She loved his positive attitude and appreciated the change in subject. It would do no good to dwell on what couldn't be changed. "Tomorrow?"

"What time?" He acted enthusiastic, almost as if Darinda didn't exist. "I need to spend some time at the office, so after work would be best. I know it's been hard on Connor trying to pick up my slack, but he says he wants me to be as prepared as possible should Darinda show up."

Connor was a good man. "I have patients all day too. How about I tell Patsy we'll meet her at 5:15?"

He smiled then stabbed a fork into the spaghetti. "Works for me."

BLAIR HAD TO work hard to get through the day and not become totally distracted. She kept visualizing Darinda popping up in the corner of her office as soon as one of her clients left. The last thing she needed was for her anxiety to rub off on them, but it was hard to stay upbeat.

Forcing herself to think of the future, she tried to imagine the perfect place for her and Ronan to live. They didn't need a lot of space, but she longed for a porch and enough room to plant some herbs in the back yard. She could even picture little bear and wolf shifters running around in the fenced-in back yard, nipping at Ronan's heels. She sighed. He would make such a wonderful father.

When she finished with her last client, Blair waited for Ronan by the Wellness Center's front door. Exiting out the side to the alley no longer held any appeal. She'd parked in back the Monday following Vinea's memory repair, and Blair swore she could still smell the coppery scent of blood in the alley, along with the stench of gunpowder. She understood her imagination had gotten the best of her, but it seemed real to her.

Today, Ronan would be picking her up at five so they could drive together to see their possible new house. Once he arrived, he leaned over the passenger seat and pushed open the door for her. As soon as Blair climbed in, her bear started to pant.

Behave. We'll be home soon enough, she said. *We have to check out a place to live first.*

Then at least kiss him, her bear demanded.

There were times when she wished her bear would go back into hiding, as she always had sex on her mind. Blair slid closer, turned his head, and then did as her bear desired. His moan almost convinced her to call Patsy and cancel their appointment, but the realtor said this property would go fast if they didn't decide quickly.

Ronan took in his fill before leaning back. "Maybe I should pick you up from work every day." When he smiled, she fell a little more in love with him.

"If you had regular hours, I'd welcome it."

Ronan put the Jeep in gear. "Where exactly are we meeting this agent?"

"At the house," Blair gave him instructions. A few minutes later, he rounded the corner and the house came into view. Her pulse quickened. The sides were brick, and it even had a nice front porch. "It's perfect."

Ronan glanced over at her. "It is."

Patsy was waiting for them when they turned down the driveway. They both slid out and greeted her.

"I think this will be ideal for you two," she said. "It's a three-bedroom, two bath house with a garage."

Blair glanced over at Ronan. "I'm not sure we need three bedrooms."

"Sure we do," he said. "For when we have a boy and a girl."

From the way he looked almost wistful, he wanted children as much as she did. Without thinking, she placed a hand on her stomach. "There is that."

For the next twenty minutes, Patsy showed them the house. While the appliances were rather worn and the walls could use a good coat of paint, the space was perfect.

"The good news," Patsy said, "is that the owner said if you're ever interested in buying the place, he'd consider selling."

Ronan reached out, grabbed Blair's hand, and smiled. The dark goddess seemed so far off right now that Blair allowed the joy of the moment to sink in.

The rent was in their price range, and after a short discussion, they decided they wanted it. The tenant would be moving out in two weeks, and Blair just hoped they were still alive to enjoy it.

Chapter Seventeen

D ARINDA WAS CONVINCED Androf was giving her all the shit jobs to do as a punishment for messing up in Silver Lake. Otherwise, she would have returned to exact her revenge.

"I think it's time you make amends for that botched murder," Androf said out of the blue. Most likely it was because the last few jobs had been executed flawlessly if she did say so herself.

Darinda stood tall and forced a dark red aura to encompass her as a show of extreme confidence. "I will prove to you that I am far worthier than any other goddess in the realm, past and present."

Androf grinned, which pleased her to no end. "I see your hatred of Vinea still burns bright. Good. Now take care of business and don't come back until you succeed." His smile had been fake for sure.

"I won't fail."

After that little discussion, Darinda immediately sought out Cynthia, her ward. As much as Darinda had balked about having to train some newbie, she did have her uses. The girl had more or less befriended Blair when Cynthia had taken over for Eve, and while Cynthia no longer worked at the Wellness Center, if she appeared as a client, she might be able to find out what Blair and that no-good boyfriend of hers were up to. Until the moment was right, Darinda didn't want to show her face in Silver Lake.

Sure, Darinda could hover in Blair and Ronan's house to learn their plans, but of late her ability to remain invisible had been sketchy. It had been Androf's way of showing his disapproval. It didn't really matter. Once she succeeded at removing those two, she'd ask him to remove his stupid curse. Then she'd be eternally powerful.

It was time to have Cynthia do her bidding.

She found her young ward in the arena learning how to fight. Those skills were beneath a goddess of Darinda's status, but if Cynthia wanted to test her skills, so be it.

Darinda floated toward her and stepped in between her and her opponent. "I need you to do something for me."

Cynthia's eyes flashed dark, but she held her tongue. Smart girl. "What is it?"

"I need for you to find out what Blair Murdoch is up to. I want to know if she remembers anything about the little incident in the alley."

"How can I find that out?"

The girl's lack of imagination pissed her off. "Go in as a client and fucking ask her." Stupid bitch. The youth of today was so lacking.

"But I'm not injured."

Darinda smiled. "That can be arranged."

BLAIR WAS SURPRISED at the identity of her next client. She hadn't recognized Cynthia's name when Eve handed her the list but knew her as soon as Cynthia walked in. Blair smiled. "Hey, nice to see you again. Have a seat on the table. It says here, you are experiencing back pain?" Cynthia nodded. "How did you hurt yourself? And how long have you been in pain?" It couldn't have been too long since she was in good shape when she worked those few days for Eve.

Rubbing her lower back, Cynthia blew out a breath. "I injured it yesterday. I stupidly decided to take up martial arts, and someone slammed me to the mat. The pain has been excruciating."

"Ouch. Let me check that out."

Blair began pressing on different spots, and as soon as Cynthia winced, Blair had a good idea what she needed to do.

"You said you lived a few towns over, right?" Blair asked.

"Yes."

"There's no clinic there?"

Cynthia looked uncomfortable. "They were booked up, and I was hoping for some quick relief."

"I'm glad you sought help. Backs usually don't heal themselves. You're lucky you are young."

Blair had her lie on her back and pull up her knees one at a time to stretch out the muscles.

"I heard what happened in the alley," Cynthia said. "You must have nightmares."

A lot of people had asked her that. "Not really. For the longest time, I remembered nothing. I was lucky, I think."

"For the longest time?"

"Bits and pieces have slowly emerged."

She sucked in a breath, but Blair wasn't sure if it was because of her back pain or what she'd just said. "So, you saw that guy kill the drug dealer?"

Something was off about this woman. Since Ronan's father had confessed, it was best to go along with the story, but she didn't remember reading that Timothy Delahart dealt drugs. "Yes. I remember the gunshot, but then everything becomes really blurry. I hope I never remember the rest." For the remainder of the treatment, Blair remained highly professional. "You should schedule three appointments a week until the pain goes away."

Cynthia smiled. "It's a bit far for me to drive. Now that I know therapy can help, I'm going to see if I can find someone over in Crenshaw."

"Ask Eve to fax the report to your new doctor."

"Will do."

After the woman left, Blair replayed the questions in her head. If she hadn't felt the swelling in her back, she would have thought she'd made the appointment just for the gossip. Ridiculous. Darinda must be getting into her head after all.

"What did she say?" Darinda asked Cynthia.

"Blair's memory is spotty. She doesn't recall seeing anyone kill that man. All she remembers is hearing the gunshot."

"Did you believe her, or did she figure out why you were asking so many questions?"

Cynthia planted a hand on her hip. "I was careful. Trust me."

She didn't trust her one bit. "You are dismissed."

That was a wasted trip. As soon as Cynthia left, Darinda skulked around, waiting to see if Androf would need her. Since he appeared to be chastising another goddess, she took off so she could see for herself what was going on. When she'd erased Blair's and Ronan's memory, it was supposed to stay erased, but she had a bad feeling about this. If Vinea had interfered, her two little friends would pay dearly with their lives.

Luckily, Blair was still at work when Darinda arrived in her invisible form. She couldn't afford to stay long, but the moment she located her target, she almost lost it. Every time Darinda interacted with a mortal, she left a bit of her signature inside them. Now that piece of her was gone—erased so to speak.

As much as she wanted to harm Vinea personally, goddesses were impossible to find if they didn't want to be located. Darinda would have to be content with harming those Vinea and her weak little mate cared for.

While she planned her revenge, Darinda shot over to McKinnon and Associates, hoping to find Ronan, only he wasn't there. Crap. It made sense that Vinea would have removed the curse from both of them. Fuck you, Vinea!

Before Androf realized she'd left, Darinda returned to the dark realm, but it wouldn't be long before she came back.

"I WAS THINKING about a Sunday picnic near the lake, and then a romp in the woods," Ronan said. "What do you think?"

"I'd love that! Work has been a little crazy, and I can certainly use the exercise. But first, I want to call Izzy to see if she can contact Ophelia for me."

"Why? She wasn't able to retrieve our memories."

"Doesn't mean she can't help. Ophelia gave Missy a powder that killed a demon on Cargonia. Maybe she has something that will slow down a goddess."

Ronan shrugged. "It can't hurt."

"I'll only be a moment."

"How about I make some peanut butter and jelly sandwiches while you make the call? That's the limit of my culinary skills."

Blair smiled. "You do make the best PB&J sandwiches."

While Ronan set about gathering the food for the picnic, she located her phone and called her friend, pleased when she answered on the first ring. "Hey, Izzy, I was wondering if you could contact Ophelia for me."

She hesitated. "I would, but she's not in town."

Blair's shoulders slumped. Damn. She might have only returned to Silver Lake three years ago, but in all that time she'd never heard of the witch leaving town. "Do you know when she'll return?"

"Within the week I suspect. Is something wrong?"

Every Murdoch and McKinnon was well aware of what had happened. "I have this terrible feeling that Darinda will be returning here soon, wanting revenge against Vinea. She might try to harm us to get back at her."

"You two are loose ends in Timothy Delahart's murder, but what were you hoping Ophelia could do?"

"She gave Missy some potion that killed the demon that was attacking Zane. I thought maybe she could help me against a goddess."

"I've never heard of anything like that. Next time I speak with Ophelia, I'll ask her what she can do."

It was all Blair could ask. "Thanks."

Ronan looked up expectantly. "Any luck?"

"No." But that setback wouldn't dampen her day. Spending time with Ronan would be wonderful. Besides, she had some incredible news to tell him, news she was sure he'd be happy to hear. "I need to change. I'll be right back."

Blair rushed off to put on some shorts and an easy-to-remove top. After a hard run, redressing was often trying, especially if her clothes were too tight. She placed a hand on her belly, wondering how long it would be before she showed. Blair could already feel some changes starting to happen. As much as she wanted to wait until she believed she could take the baby to term, it was time to let Ronan know what was in store for their future—assuming they both lived that long.

Now why did she have to think that depressing thought? The joy that she'd been filled with a moment ago evaporated. Blair glanced at the ceiling. "Why can't you leave us alone, Darinda?" she whispered, not wanting Ronan to hear.

Of course, she received no response, which she decided was for the best. Blair returned to the living room where the sack with their food sat on the table next to a blanket.

"You're hot," he said with a familiar gleam in his eye.

She grinned then wagged a finger at him, "I know that look— picnic first—then playtime." She wanted to break the news to him about the baby before anything else. Then she wanted to discuss mating.

Ronan chuckled, a sound that had been all too absent in the house as of late. "Spoilsport."

The drive to Silver Lake was mercifully short. The sun shone brilliantly, the sky was a deep cerulean blue, and the delicate breeze would help keep the flies away.

Once they arrived, Ronan slung his sword over his shoulder and picked up a shield, along with the bag of food. Blair apparently was in charge of the blanket.

She nodded to the shield. "When did you get that?"

"Zane just made it for me. He said he was able to add some special elements that would repel my opponent's blows. He wasn't positive it would work against a goddess, but it had been effective against a demon.

"Can I see how heavy it is?" she asked.

"Sure." He handed it to her and grabbed the blanket she was carrying.

"Not bad. I like it." It was a lot lighter than she expected. When she held it in front, she tripped on a root but caught herself. "You better take this."

Ronan smiled. "It's best to leave the battling to the man."

When he stuck out his chest, she laughed. "Why are you taking it with you to a picnic?"

"I want to practice using the shield with the sword. I suspect my balance will be off having both. Don't worry, you get to sit back and watch your hot man practice his smooth moves."

She chuckled. "I do enjoy any reason to watch, and I thank you for waiting until you have room to practice." The one and only time he had tried to demonstrate his expertise in the house, he'd broken a decorative plate.

A few minutes later, they arrived at the clearing, and she was thankful no one had the same idea about a picnic.

"How about this spot?" Ronan said, setting down his gear.

"Perfect."

"It was right around here that you found my bear for me," she said.

"I did?" Ronan acted all innocent. "Hmm. Maybe I did." A second later she was in his arms enjoying a warm and wonderful kiss.

Blair might not have stopped had her stomach not grumbled. "Sorry."

"I'm hungry too. How about we eat and then take advantage of the wonderful day?"

"Sounds divine."

Once he spread out the blanket, she emptied the contents of the bag. He'd packed four bottles of water, three sandwiches, and two bags of chips. It was such a guy picnic. Before she had polished off half of the sandwich, a red glowing object materialized to her right. When she looked directly at the light, a body of woman appeared, and Blair's heart took a major jolt. "Ronan," Blair said, her voice cracking. "We have company."

Faster than she thought possible, Ronan jumped to his feet and grabbed his sword. "Darinda."

Chapter Eighteen

"WELL, WELL, LOOKIE who is here." Darinda grinned and stepped closer.

"Blair," Ronan growled. "Go back to the car."

That wasn't going to happen. "No."

"Don't argue. Please."

Not wanting to distract him, she stepped back a few feet, searching for something she could use to harm the goddess. Her muscles were close to mush, and her brain was becoming scrambled, but she looked around anyway. It was almost as if Darinda was sending out signals to interfere with her thought process. Blair could only hope the goddess didn't try to erase their memories again since they needed to remember that this goddess was someone who wanted to destroy them.

Blair picked up a rock, but she doubted it would do any good. Now she wished she had asked Vinea more questions about what kind of things could hurt someone like Darinda.

The dark goddess cackled. "Oh, Blair. You are so charming. Do you really think that little pebble can harm me? I am immortal, you know." She glanced over at Ronan, her eyes widening. "My, what a big sword you have. Too bad it won't do you any good against me, but it will be cute to see you try."

Ronan unsheathed his sword and swung it overhead, looking powerful and in control.

Darinda clapped. "Oh, this is going to be such fun," she said with so much cheer in her voice, it scared Blair even more.

A second later, a wolf emerged from behind the goddess, looking exactly like Ronan. This animal had the same brown snout, even down to the distinctive white patch under his right eye.

"Do you like?" Darinda asked, almost acting flirty. What the hell was up with that? "This is Nanor, your double." She smiled. "In case you aren't thinking straight, I named him Nanor because it's Ronan spelled backward." Her laugh sounded so evil. "His skills match yours, only he's a bit stronger, faster, and has a lot more endurance. And if you injure him, he'll heal immediately." She pressed her palms together, probably trying to look pious. That was a joke.

"Here are the rules," Darinda continued. "Kill Nanor and I'll let you fight me. Not that you'll live past today regardless of how you handle yourself with this magnificent beast, but it will bring me much joy to see the life slowly drain out of you." The goddess glanced over at Blair. "As for you, my dear, I will take great pleasure in watching you see your mate suffer. Once he is gone, I am going to have my fun with you too."

Vomit rolled up her throat, and this time it wasn't from the baby growing inside her. "Ronan will kill you," she spat.

"That will never happen." She looked back at Ronan. "I suggest you shift, unless you want Nanor to tear you apart right now."

The beast's eyes were black with red irises that radiated pure evil. Blair wanted to rush over to Ronan and hug and kiss him one last time, but he didn't even glance her way. She had to believe it was because he didn't want to become distracted.

Slowly and methodically, he undressed and then tossed his clothes to the side, almost as if he expected to be putting them back on at some point in time.

There had to be something she could do, but what? Shift? She was a bear with long claws. She could do damage to a little wolf, though she doubted Darinda would let her get that close. This was Ronan's fight.

Once naked, Ronan shifted, and except for the color of the

doppelganger's eyes, even Blair couldn't tell them apart. Crouching low, Ronan attempted to circle his opponent, but before he was halfway around, Nanor leaped into the air and landed on Ronan's back. When the alien wolf sunk his teeth into his back, Ronan let out a high-pitched shriek, and Blair's pulse shot into overdrive. The resulting gaping gash horrified her.

Do something, her bear begged.

Let's see what Ronan does next. We can step in if we need to, but I don't think Darinda will allow that. Blair had witnessed quite a few fights in her life and the outcome wasn't determined by one or two swipes. It took time to kill a wolf.

As if Ronan sensed her encouragement, he wrestled the fake wolf to the ground, clawing at its side. *Go, go, go*, her bear urged.

Nanor growled, seemingly injured, and Blair shouted, "You can do it, Ronan."

As if her voice helped motivated him, Ronan lifted his head, and aimed for the wolf's neck. Whether or not this wolf could even die was anyone's guess. Vinea never said anything about there being wolves in the dark realm.

Focused on the fight, Blair jerked and moved with every swipe of Nanor's paw. When the opponent scraped his claws across Ronan's snout, Blair could almost feel his pain. Ronan stumbled as blood spurted out of the side of his face. The animal attacked again, this time digging his teeth closer to Ronan's throat. It was almost as if this Darinda-driven animal was toying with him, wanting the fight to cause as much pain as possible.

By some miracle, Ronan managed to throw off his opponent. He struggled to stand, but even when on all fours, Ronan was unable to keep his balance very well, teetering and breathing heavily. Blair ached for him, and for their baby who might never know his father.

Despite his wounds, Ronan seemed determined to win. With teeth bared, he charged, clawing at his opponent's legs and then digging his teeth into the animal's neck.

"That's it, Ronan. He's going down."

The red eyed monster staggered then inexplicably revived. He crawled toward Ronan as if he believed that by keeping low, he'd have the advantage.

Blair couldn't stand to watch any longer. The lookalike was some kind of super wolf. Just like Darinda claimed, he wasn't tiring at all. Needing to help, Blair shifted into her bear form, stood on her hind legs, and growled.

"Oh, my," Darinda said, not looking concerned at all. "You are a big one, aren't you?"

She'd show Darinda just how big. Blair dropped to all fours and charged. Before she reached the two wolves trying to claim each other's lives, a force, the strength of which Blair had never experienced before, knocked her back a good twenty feet. She landed on her butt before hitting her head against a tree trunk.

What the hell?

"Don't interfere again, or I will kill you," Darinda said, her voice turning low and full of hatred.

The goddess was going to kill her regardless of the outcome of this fight, so Blair might as well try again. And she would too—just as soon as her stomach stopped hurting and she was able to stand.

The two wolves snapped, bit, and clawed at each other, but Nanor didn't seem to be making as much progress as he had at first. The bad news was that every time Ronan managed to get in a good swipe, Nanor healed himself almost instantly, whereas Ronan was bloodied and growing weaker by the minute.

Blair had to help somehow. She rolled to her side and managed to rise on all fours. She then lumbered closer. If she thought shifting back to her human form would help, she would have. About ten feet from the fray, she spotted a pointed rock about four inches in diameter. She positioned it near her rear right paw, and as soon as Ronan was on the far side, she turned around and kicked the rock backward, pretending it was unintentional.

While she had no expectations of hitting the red-eyed wolf, it might distract him enough to give Ronan a chance to attack.

Before she could turn around to see if her strategy had worked, loud shrieks rent the air. Blair spun around. Ronan must have used the last ounce of his energy to fly through the air, his mouth aimed perfectly at the doppelganger's neck. As if the two were suspended in air for the longest time, Ronan's opponent finally fell, and Ronan collapsed on top of the downed wolf. Either he couldn't move, or Ronan wanted to be sure all life had drained from his enemy before disengaging. Only when Darinda started to clap, did Ronan look up. "Congratulations, Ronan. Excellent job. I am so going to enjoy killing you myself."

Blair wanted to rip out her throat. It didn't matter; it would do no good. Darinda would never die. Blair growled her displeasure. She wouldn't be surprised to learn the goddess had placed some spell on Nanor, preventing him from finishing Ronan off just so she could have the honors.

Ronan finally released his grip on the wolf's neck. Even though Nanor appeared to be dead, he didn't turn into a human after death, proving this creature was no ordinary wolf—or one from this realm.

Blair moved toward Ronan wanting to lick his wounds, but as she neared, she felt what could only be described as a bolt of electricity shooting through her, paralyzing her muscles.

The impact threw her backward again, and unimaginable pain sliced through, catching her belly on fire. The baby! No-ooo. A wave of protection swelled inside her. She would not lose this child.

While catching her breath, Blair became more determined than ever to help. She needed to have a better plan than just charging in and hoping for a good outcome.

Ronan shifted into his human form, and the horror of his appearance took her breath away. His bloodied face was a mass of scrapes and contusions, some so severe, she was uncertain if he could ever heal. His leg had a wide gash running down its length, and his shoulder was swollen and sat at an odd angle.

Somehow, he managed to come toward her, his gait uneven. Before he reached her, Darinda must have shot a bolt of the electricity through him too, for he stumbled to his knees and lowered his head. His back heaved, and Blair's hatred swelled.

The dark goddess barked out a laugh then quickly sobered. "Did I say you could go to your woman?"

Ronan looked up, his eyes blacker than black. Even in excruciating pain, he managed to mouth, "I love you."

Tears welled in her eyes. As much as Blair wanted to say the words back to him, she didn't dare, not with Darinda watching.

"Come, come now," Darinda taunted. "You still have to fight me."

Ronan grunted then stood, drawing himself up to his full height. Given the immense pain he was experiencing and the bit of fear skating across his face, it must have taken every ounce of control to stand tall. He looked over his shoulder at Darinda. "May I have a minute?"

"No. Fight me like the coward I know you are."

As if she'd held a flame to his cuts, Ronan sneered, ran a few feet to the blanket, and dove for the sword.

Darinda laughed. "That puny thing won't do you any good."

Blair almost smiled. Let the bitch underestimate him. While any normal person would say Blair was crazy for thinking Ronan had a chance, she had to believe. As she watched him grab his shield and sword, her muscles regained some of their function. Not wanting to let Darinda know she would be at full strength soon, Blair remained still, willing all of her strength into Ronan.

He glanced over at Blair. "I'm begging you. Hide."

EVERY ONE OF Ronan's muscles screamed in agony. His left leg had been seriously injured, and his right arm was weak from the shoulder damage. He wasn't even sure how he was able to stand, let alone fight a goddess, but fight he would. When he watched Darinda send Blair tumbling, his anger knew no bounds. It was what had kept him alive.

His lookalike had amazing skills and lightning fast reflexes. It had been so frustrating that the animal had been able to anticipate his every move, almost as if he'd tapped into his mind. Only by blanking his thoughts and working on instinct alone, had Ronan been able to surprise the animal and kill him. But it was Blair's kicked rock that had done the trick by distracting the animal long enough for Ronan to have the upper hand.

"What are you waiting for, Ronan?" Darinda said with her legs wide apart and her arms lifted to chest level, ready to defend herself.

Ronan wasn't sure what Zane had done to the shield or how he'd done it, but he said it contained an extra dose of magic to help him. He prayed his friend had been telling the truth.

Focus on the neck.

Ronan had practiced swinging the sword over his head for hours, but most of the time he used two hands. With a shield in one hand, his timing wasn't what he wanted it to be. His bum shoulder screamed in pain, but he forced himself to ignore his discomfort. If he died, so would Blair, and he couldn't let that happen.

Knowing his strength wouldn't last much longer, he charged. Darinda held up a hand to forestall the advance. Anticipating she'd use some kind of force against him, he raised his shield to protect himself, but a blast knocked him on his ass nonetheless. Then something strange happened. Darinda staggered backward, her face in a grimace.

Encouraged by the shield's ability to deflect part of her powers back at her, Ronan jumped to his feet. Out of the corner of his eye, he spotted Blair ducking behind one of the boulders, hiding as he'd requested. He wished she'd leave all together, but even if she managed to escape this time, Darinda would eventually find her.

Pushing aside that terrible thought, he lifted his sword again. The only way to succeed was to get close to the goddess, and that seemed like an impossible chore.

"Nice little shield you have," Darinda said. "I'm not worried though. You'll tire a lot sooner than I will." She shot another blast at him, and Ronan went sprawling once more.

Somehow, Darinda managed to dodge most of the reflected blast this time. His only hope was to outsmart her—if that was even possible. Ronan wanted her to think he couldn't go on, that he was ready to give up so he remained on the ground and caught his breath. Colors of midnight blue and deep maroon swirled around her. That combination he'd never forget—it was the sign of pure evil.

Darinda eased toward him. "You're not going to give up that easily are you? I expected more from you."

When she leaned over to check on him, he lifted up on his knees and swung the sword as hard and as accurately as he could. The blade hit her neck, but she managed to lean to the side quickly enough to avoid losing her head. As if he'd crossed some invisible line, Darinda's face turned red, and her eyes glowed the same color.

She dragged her hand over the wound and snarled. Ronan never would have believed she'd bleed red. It almost made her human.

"You will pay," she snarled, baring her teeth.

With a strong kick, she hit his wrist and sent the sword flying a good fifteen feet. As he scrambled to stand, his pulse pounded, and adrenaline soared through him. Just as he was about to make a mad dash for the sword, Blair eased out from behind the rocks.

Ronan only had one option. He held up his shield and faced Blair, forcing Darinda to turn her back on the advancing bear. "How about fighting me hand to hand?" Ronan tossed his shield to the side.

Darinda sneered. "Just because I'm a woman doesn't mean I can't beat you." She hauled off and punched him hard.

In as many brawls as he'd been in, no punch had been harder. Her fist sliced open his cheek further, but he didn't drop to his knees. He refused to give her the satisfaction.

"I'd like to see you try," he said with as much confidence as he could muster.

Darinda just laughed. Quicker than the speed of light, she attacked again.

Chapter Nineteen

B LAIR'S MUSCLES LOCKED. Her hope had soared when Ronan had been able to repel the goddess' attack with Zane's magic-filled shield. Then he stumbled in seeming agony. Only after she realized his fall was a ploy to draw Darinda closer did her fear lessen.

As much as Blair wanted to call out to him for encouragement, she didn't want Darinda to take revenge on him for her actions.

Right before Darinda kicked away his sword, Ronan had lifted up, looking like some Phoenix rising from the ashes. He'd swung his sword, connecting with her neck. How Darinda managed to duck and avoid losing her head, Blair would never understand. Then when Darinda kicked Ronan's sword right out of his hand and sent it flying, Blair nearly collapsed.

He was doomed unless she did something.

Ronan had slowly risen to his feet, spat on the ground, and then tossed down his shield. Blair's heart stopped. What was he doing?

Get the sword, her bear urged.

Wait a minute. That sounded like Ronan's voice in her head, not her bear's, or was she hallucinating? She had to be since they hadn't mated.

I've never swung a sword in my life, she mentally responded, hoping for some guidance—only none came.

When the sunlight glinted off the steel, it was almost as if some goddess of the light was giving her a signal to defend them. Blair shifted into her human form. Totally exposed and highly vulnerable, she edged closer to the weapon. Darinda knocked Ronan down once more, and this time it was no ploy when he remained on his knees. Ronan was losing strength fast.

Blair waited for a wink, a shout, or eye contact to tell her it was time to fight, but none came. *Get up, Ronan,* she urged. *I don't know if I can do this.*

When Darinda slammed her foot into Ronan's chest, his eyes bugged out and his mouth gaped opened. A wave of anger blasted Blair. Without thinking, she picked up the weapon and lifted it over her head. Ronan thrust his leg outward, connecting with Darinda's shin, and then he growled.

"You won't win." His shout was loud—loud enough to block out Blair's approach.

Now. Do it now.

Petrified and horrified, Blair stood to her full height and ran toward Darinda, sword wavering. Ronan must have glanced her way or else the goddess possessed a sixth sense because Darinda's shoulder rotated. In one second, she'd be facing Blair.

It was now or never.

With a force she didn't know she possessed, Blair brought the blade down as hard as she could. The impact with Darinda's neck sickened her, but Blair didn't let up on the pressure. Her momentum carried the blade through the bones, the skin, and the body. When the bloodied sword emerged on the other side, the realization of what she'd done was so horrible that she dropped the weapon and stepped back.

Darinda's head landed on the dirt, and her body followed. Then, as if she had never been there, the goddess evaporated. A second later, her wolf Nanor disappeared too.

Stunned, Blair crashed to her knees next to Ronan. She expected him to rise, embrace her, and tell her everything would be okay. Only he didn't move.

Blair crawled to his side and shook him. "Ronan? Darinda is dead. She can't hurt you anymore. Wake up."

When he remained still, she pressed her fingers to his neck to check for a pulse. Between her own heart pounding hard and the pool of blood covering the side of his face, she couldn't tell if he was breathing or not. "Ronan!"

Think. Think.

She wished he could shift back and heal himself, but until he roused, he wouldn't be able to change into his wolf form. It was up to her to save him. Stopping the bleeding had to be her first task. Even though the picnic supplies were strewn everywhere, Blair located a full water bottle jammed up against one of the rocks near the lake. She opened it and held it against his lips. "Ronan, drink this."

When his lips didn't move and his head lolled to the side, her stomach tumbled. He couldn't die. She wouldn't let him.

Wanting to make him comfortable, Blair rolled up the blanket and placed it under his head. Next, she poured the water over the worst of his cuts, and then tore his shirt into strips to make bandages. Dirt had filled the wounds, and if he didn't shift soon, he might lose a limb.

Once she carefully wrapped the cloth around his upper thighs as well as around the wound in his arm, she poured the rest of the water on the remaining material and cleaned his face the best she could. No matter how hard she pressed or what she did, he never moaned, never moved.

"Ronan Laramie, you will not die. Do you hear me?" Her blood pressure skyrocketed. "Please, Ronan, don't you want to hold your son or daughter?"

Though after what she'd been through, it would be a miracle if the baby survived. Damn it. There had to be more she could do.

Missy. She could help. Only Blair had left her phone in the car. As much as she didn't want to leave him, she had to call for help. She'd done all she could for him.

Blair quickly dressed, located his keys in his pants pocket, and took off. At the Jeep, she called Missy and explained what happened and then begged her to come to the lake.

"I'll call Zane. We'll be there as fast as we can," Missy promised.

"Thank you."

Blair wasn't sure who else could help, so she called Jackson. Her brother answered. "Ronan! You ever coming back to work?" His cheer made it hard to respond.

Blair almost broke down. "It's me, Jackson. Ronan is injured." Just retelling what happened traumatized her further. "I already called Missy, and she's on her way."

"Good. I'll be right there. Stay with him."

Blair disconnected and hurried back to the lake. Her back ached, and her headache was worsening by the minute, but she ran as fast as she could. Slamming against the tree trunk after being tossed backward by Darinda's powers might have given her a concussion, but right now she couldn't even remember if she'd lost consciousness. It didn't matter. What was important was saving Ronan.

When she returned, he hadn't moved, though his bandages were soaked, which was both good and bad. It was bad because he was losing blood, but good that it meant he was still alive.

She sat next to him. "Ronan? Can you hear me?"

Sweat beaded on his forehead. When his fingers twitched, she sucked in a breath, hoping he was arousing. She placed a hand on his wrist, one of the few areas that hadn't been injured and squeezed gently. "Wake up, please. I need you."

His leg twitched, and then his head lolled from side to side. While nothing she said seemed to wake him, at least he was breathing. Every few seconds, Blair glanced to the path, hoping to see Missy and Zane. After what seemed like hours had passed, leaves rustled and then two figures appeared.

Missy and Zane rushed toward them. "How is he?" Zane asked, clearly fearful for his friend's life.

"Not good."

"Blair, I need some room to work," Missy said.

"Of course."

Zane helped Blair up and walked her over to the shade. "Tell me what happened. You said you killed the goddess?"

If she hadn't been so upset, she would have found some pride in his disbelief. "Yes."

She'd just finished detailing the fight, from the lookalike animal to the actual battle with Darinda, when Jackson arrived. She'd never been so happy to see him.

He hugged her. "How are you?"

Blair wasn't up for discussing her injuries. "I'm okay."

"I'll see how Missy is fairing," Zane said. "You can bring Jackson up to speed."

Her brother gathered her in his arms. "It sounds like it was such a terrible ordeal, but Ronan will be okay."

He couldn't know that, but she appreciated his optimism. By the time she detailed the events again, Zane and Missy returned.

"I've done all I can," Missy said. "What he needs now is to rest."

"Should we call a doctor?" It wasn't that she didn't trust Missy, but Blair didn't want to leave any stone unturned.

Jackson wrapped an arm around her shoulder. "When he wakes up, we'll see what his wolf can do. You know as well as I do that explaining where the claw marks came from would be difficult if we take him to a hospital."

She knew of a few shifter doctors she could ask for help. "I'll wait two days and no longer."

Jackson nodded. She and Missy picked up what was left of the picnic, along with Ronan's clothes, and then followed Zane and Jackson, who were carrying Ronan, back to the car. Zane was so large he probably could have carried Ronan all by himself.

Because Zane insisted he drive Ronan's Jeep, Blair went with Jackson who made an unconscious Ronan comfortable in the back of his vehicle. Missy followed so she could then drive Zane home from Blair's.

Once there, the men carried Ronan into the bedroom. Missy placed her hands on Ronan's forehead and said some chant designed, she'd claimed, to draw out Darinda's evil.

A half hour later, Missy and Zane left. Jackson said he would stay, but Blair insisted on being alone with the man she loved.

"Call me if you need me," Jackson said.

"I will." After a quick hug, he left.

Blair dragged one of the dining room chairs into the bedroom and sat, ready for the vigil. Her own body needed rest, but Ronan needed her more.

After three hours, Ronan didn't seem to be any better, and she wondered if his wounds should be cleaned a little better. If only his wolf would take over, he'd improve quickly.

Before she had the chance to check, someone knocked on her front door, and Blair debated not answering. If she had to go through the story once more, she might be scarred for life.

"Blair, it's Ainsley!"

Ainsley. Just hearing her best friend's voice perked her up. Pushing on her knees to stand, her back screamed, but she stood anyway. Every muscle craved rest. When her stomach grumbled, she realized she had to eat, if only for the baby's sake.

Blair opened the door to find more than just her friend. Ainsley had brought the twins! Without thinking, her hand shot to her stomach. Jackson was there along with Dr. Bill Hardy, a bear shifter physician. Relief that Ronan would get some medical help filled her. "Come in."

As much as Blair wanted to spend time with the newborns, she needed to consult with Dr. Hardy first.

He lifted a black leather bag. "I don't normally make house calls, but Jackson told me Ronan is in bad shape."

"Yes. Come with me." She glanced over at her brother and his mate.

Ainsley held up a hand. "Go. We'll be fine."

They headed into the bedroom. "Has he shown any signs of improvement?" the doctor asked.

"Not really. His hands and legs twitch every now and again, but he hasn't opened his eyes, and he doesn't respond to me talking to him."

"I'll want to take a look at the wounds. You said it was a wolf that attacked him?"

"Yes." She doubted Jackson had mentioned the goddess.

"I may be awhile." Dr. Hardy didn't move, clearly wanting to be alone with Ronan.

"Of course." She returned to the living room just as Jackson was bringing in a folding cot. "What's that for?" she asked.

Ainsley led her over to the sofa. "Sit down. We need to talk."

Blair knew that tone. "About what?"

Her best friend clasped her hands. She then turned back to Jackson who was unfolding the cot. "Can you get the food out of the truck too?" Ainsley asked him.

"Sure."

"Food? Cot? What's going on?"

"I can see the signs," Ainsley said.

"Signs?" Blair could figure out where this was headed.

"How far along are you?"

Her pulse fluttered. "I don't know how you knew, but I'm about six weeks pregnant."

"I've happy for you, but that's all the more reason why you need to rest and eat. You know what happened the last time you let stress get to you?"

She didn't need the reminder. Blair lived with it every day. "I know."

"Did I hear someone is expecting?" Jackson asked, his cheer evident.

"Yes, but don't tell Ronan. I want to surprise him." *Assuming the baby survives.*

Jackson rushed over and hugged her. "Congrats and my lips are sealed."

She had the best family in the world.

"When the doc finishes up with Ronan, we need to ask him to

check you out," Ainsley said.

"I actually would feel better if he made sure the baby is okay."

Ainsley pulled a piece of paper from her purse and handed it to Blair. "I've made a few calls and set up a schedule. I know you want to watch Ronan twenty-four seven, but it won't do either of you any good if you collapse, so members of both families will be taking turns standing watch. Of course, Sam and Lexi will take shifts too, as will the rest of the firm."

The support and love overwhelmed her, bringing her to tears. Damn hormones. She hugged Ainsley. "Did I tell you how much I love you?"

Ainsley leaned back, her cheeks red. "You can prove it by doing as I ask. The cot is going to be for you when you need your rest. And I don't want to hear any arguments."

Blair didn't know what to say. "Thank you. I hope Ronan is back to normal in a few days."

Jackson came in again bearing a box from Nathan's pizza. "From the looks of the picnic, you didn't have a chance to eat."

"No, I didn't. Thank you," Blair said.

When the doctor emerged from the bedroom, his face appeared grim. "I've changed his bandages, and the wounds appear to be healing, so I'm not sure what is causing his lack of response."

Blair jumped up. "What can I do?"

"Keep doing what you're doing. Talk to him to see if you can get him to respond. If he's not improved in a few days, call me. I'll give you some antibiotics for him to take once he wakes, though if he can shift into his wolf form that should cure him faster than any pills will. Because he will need to stay hydrated, I'll stop by tomorrow with some saline solution."

She didn't like the prognosis. "Thank you."

Ainsley stood. "Blair?"

She nodded. "Do you think you could take a look at my injuries?" She explained how she'd slammed against a rock.

"What Blair hasn't mentioned is that she is six weeks pregnant."

The doctor's eyes widened. "Of course. Come back to the bedroom and I'll check you out."

After a thorough exam—or as thorough as was possible given the lack of equipment, he said that with rest, both she and the baby should be okay. Relief washed through her.

Once she thanked him for everything, the doctor left. Blair turned her attention to the twins—one boy and one girl. Ainsley was so lucky.

"Would you like to hold Sarah?" she asked. "Or Jake? You should practice, you know."

As if the last few weeks never existed, she held out her arms and Ainsley handed her Sarah, and every motherly instinct she had soared. The baby smelled of talcum powder and pure sweetness. When Sarah cooed and then smiled, Blair's heart sang.

As if Jackson lived there, he brought over some plates for the pizza, along with bottles for the babies, "Time to eat."

Blair wanted to check on Ronan again, but she'd hear him if he awakened. For the next half hour, they ate and chatted about the twins—their eating habits, how much they slept, and how little sleep Ainsley and Jackson had each night. Blair yawned.

"You need to rest, sis." Jackson rolled the bed down the hallway, where Blair was instructed to rest.

While he watched the kids, she and Ainsley changed the sheets on the cot. Blair didn't think she'd be able to sleep, but as soon as Ainsley returned to the living room, it was lights out for her.

To her surprise, she awoke rather refreshed. When she stepped into the living room, the babies were sound asleep and so was Ainsley.

"You should take Ainsley and the kids, home," she whispered. "They could use the rest too."

Jackson nodded. "I will."

Ainsley opened her eyes and sat up. "Hey, did you sleep?" she asked Blair.

She managed a smile. "Yes, thanks to you. I'm good to watch

Ronan now."

"Okay. Your father will be stopping in tomorrow at nine to watch Ronan for a bit," Ainsley said.

"Thanks for everything. It means so much to me." She wanted to say it wasn't necessary for everyone to pitch in, but arguing would fall on deaf ears.

Once they left, she turned on one of Ronan's favorite shows, pretending he was awake and sitting next to her. He was going to wake up. He had to.

Chapter Twenty

THE NEXT WEEK was a total blur. People came and people went, but Ronan didn't improve much. Yes, his wounds looked better, but no matter how much Blair talked to him, he never responded.

She finally had to call Dr. Hardy, who said he'd stop by after he finished with his patients. After checking on Ronan, the doctor shook his head. "I've never seen anything like this in my life. His wolf seems to be dormant. The wounds are almost healed, so I see no reason why he's not up and around. I'll leave you a few more bags of saline, but you might consider contacting a witch."

"A witch?"

"You need help beyond my expertise."

Blair's legs weakened, and her stomach churned, but she was determined to find answers. "Thank you."

As soon as he left, she called Izzy who answered immediately. "Is Ronan awake?"

"No." She explained about the doctor's visit and what he suggested. "He has no idea why Ronan hasn't responded. Darinda must have done something to him during the fight. That's why I really need to speak with Ophelia."

"She returned last night. I'll try to convince her to make a house call."

Relief washed through her. "That would be fantastic."

"I think you're right in asking her."

"Thanks. Ronan is strong, and only something as powerful as a curse could keep him down."

"I'll call you back after I make contact," Izzy said.

Tears welled up in her eyes at the support. "You are the best."

"Back at you."

Once they disconnected, Blair checked on Ronan again. She placed a palm on his forehead to check for a fever, but he didn't have a temperature. His wounds looked good, his breathing appeared strong, and except for the saline drip, he looked healthy. Okay, his beard could use a trim, but other than that, he was her Ronan—or at least he would be as soon as he awoke.

Izzy called a few minutes later to say she'd contacted the powerful witch. Within an hour, Izzy arrived with the wonderful Ophelia in tow. Blair showed them in. "I can't tell you how much I appreciate this, Ophelia."

"Nonsense. I've been having this foreboding for the last few days, and I can see now it was because of Ronan."

Blair wasn't sure if that was a good thing or not. "Can you help him?"

She gave her a brief smile. "I'll try."

Blair and Izzy sat on the sofa while Ophelia did her thing alone in the bedroom. Fifteen minutes later, she stepped out of the bedroom. "I can feel the dark force inside him. I can't even tell you what the curse is, but I need help to get rid of it."

Blair grabbed Izzy's hand and squeezed. "What are you saying—that he'll never wake up?"

Ophelia held her gaze steady. "No, I need to join forces with someone else who has a particular kind of magical healing touch."

"Do you have someone in mind?"

"Yes. I know a man. Declan Sinclair is a healer on Tarradon."

Her breath caught. "Tarradon? Where Finn is?" She almost hyperventilated at the hopeless situation.

"Yes." Ophelia moved to Blair's other side and placed a hand on her leg, sending what felt like a healing warmth that flowed throughout her body, helping to calm her breathing. "I will contact him," she said.

"You're sure he can help?"

"Declan is very powerful. Together, we can heal him, assuming he is free to make the trip."

"Can't you make him come here?"

"My dear, I am but an old lady. He owes me a few favors however." She winked. "I think I can convince him."

A trickle of hope edged in like a root trying to gain purchase in a rock crevice. "Thank you."

"It will take time to set this up."

Blair grabbed Ophelia's hand. "Please hurry."

"Don't worry. Now, if you will help me up, I shall be on my way." Blair stood and guided Ophelia to her feet and then hugged Izzy.

Once they left, Blair's energy improved. Ophelia had been known to solve many problems in Silver Lake, but did her powers extend to other realms?

She wouldn't be any good to Ronan or the baby if she didn't eat. Blair was halfway through making lunch when Ronan's sister arrived for her shift.

"How is he?" Lexi asked with her fingers laced together.

As much as Blair appreciated all of the concern, telling everyone that there had been no change depressed her. "The same, but there is some good news."

"What is that?"

Blair could tell that Lexi was trying not to become too excited. "Ophelia stopped by and said she might know of someone who can help him."

"Really, who?"

"Someone from a different realm," She explained about what the witch had told her. "But keep it to yourself. I don't want the others to expect a miracle."

"That's great. I'm going to check on him. Why don't you finish eating and rest? I'll stay with him for a while."

THE NEXT FOUR days were torture waiting for Ophelia to let her know whether this Declan healer could help out or not.

"Sit down, Blair, please. You're driving me crazy. I'm betting Ronan can sense your nervousness too," Chelsea McKinnon said.

She was right. "You know, if Declan does come, you could ask him how Finn is doing."

Her eyes sparkled. "That would be amazing. After all, Declan is Finn's mate's brother."

Finn's departure to Tarradon might have hit his twin the hardest. Even Blair had seen the change in his sister. Chelsea had been so upbeat and happy until the day Finn left. Yes, Finn and his mate had returned once, but Chelsea said they'd only been able to stay a day.

"Can I refresh your drink?" Blair asked.

"Sure."

Blair had just reached the kitchen when someone rang the front door bell. Her mom wasn't scheduled to come over for another two hours. Blair answered the door and froze. Tiny Ophelia was standing next to a giant. His dark hair was crew cut short, and his shoulders were so wide she wondered if he could fit through her door. Even before Ophelia introduced her guest, Blair had to assume he was the dragon shifter, Declan Sinclair.

"Come in." She tried to smile, but the muscles around her mouth wouldn't move.

Ophelia looked over at Chelsea and smiled before returning her gaze to Blair. "This is the healer I mentioned—Declan Sinclair."

Blair held out her hand. "I can't thank you enough for coming."

"I'd like to begin my work, if you don't mind."

A bit distant, perhaps, but quite professional. She liked that. "Of course."

As soon as he looked over at Chelsea, his eyes turned a beautiful teal color. What was that about? He headed straight toward her.

"You must be Chelsea, Finn's twin."

"Yes."

"The resemblance is remarkable."

Chelsea's face reddened. "I guess we do kind of look alike, though Finn's hair is much darker."

"True. I'd love to chat a bit when I finish with Ronan." He turned to Ophelia. "Shall we?"

"The bedroom is the first door on the right," Blair said, even though Ophelia knew where it was.

Together, the two disappeared into the room. As much as Blair wanted to watch them, she sensed Ophelia wanted to be alone with the healer.

"Tea! I was making you some tea."

Happy to have something to do, she ducked into the kitchen and put the water on to boil.

"I can't believe Finn's mate's brother is actually here."

"I know, right?"

Before she and Chelsea finished their drink, the bedroom door opened and Declan and Ophelia returned. Blair jumped up, her fists clenched. "Well?"

Declan glanced over at Chelsea and smiled. He then turned back to Blair. "Your man should be up and around soon. With Ophelia's help, I was able to withdraw the curse. I have to say your goddess was quite powerful."

"Darinda sure was." She wanted to hug the man, but when Ophelia threaded an arm around his, Blair refrained. "I can't thank you all enough," Blair said.

"You're welcome. I wish I could stay and see if Earth has changed since I was here last, but I just received a message that I am needed on Tarradon." He looked over at Chelsea. "Maybe we'll meet again."

Chelsea beamed. "I'd like that. Hopefully, I can persuade my brother to give me a tour of Tarradon."

"I'll be happy to convince Finn to do so."

"We must go," Ophelia said, tugging on Declan's arm.

Chelsea rushed up to him. "Finn is okay, isn't he?"

He chuckled, and Chelsea's eyes lit up. "Your brother is fine—as is my sister. The two of them are doing very well indeed, but I can tell that he misses you terribly."

Chelsea clasped his other arm, and Declan's face softened. What an interesting reaction.

Blair pictured what it would be like to have Ronan open his eyes and look at her that way again.

"I miss him so much. Tell him I love him," Chelsea said.

Declan smiled down at Chelsea, and Blair could almost see her swoon. "I will."

"I need to get this young man back home," Ophelia said.

As quickly as they came, they left. Chelsea faced her. "Wasn't he amazing?"

Her excitement was almost contagious. "Yes. He certainly is larger than life."

Chelsea giggled. "He is. I can't tell you what just talking with someone who knows Finn means to me." She sagged. "I wish I could make a visit. From what Finn said the last time he was here, traveling through the portal only takes a second."

Poor Chelsea missed him so much. "When he can, I bet he'll invite you for a visit."

"I hope so." Her voice trailed off.

Blair wanted to spend more time with Chelsea, but she also wanted to check on Ronan. "Why don't you go and tell your family the good news about Finn?"

"You don't want me to stay?"

"You heard the man. Ronan will be up and around shortly." She hugged Chelsea.

"Okay, but I'll be expecting a visit from Ronan soon."

She smiled. "I'll be sure to tell him." As soon as Chelsea left, Blair dashed into the bedroom. Because he was still out, Blair crawled into bed, ready to greet him when he awoke.

Chapter Twenty-One

C OLORFUL SWIRLS PAINTED the back of his lids. Ronan twisted then jerked, but his body was unable to coordinate his muscles. As much as he wanted to open his eyes, they didn't seem to be obeying his command. The aches and heaviness that had plagued him seemed to have let loose, but he would still have to fight to regain consciousness.

Wait a minute. Blair was near! The pinks and purples were awash with tension-filled grays though, adding to his concern.

Without trying, his bones cracked and his body transformed into his wolf.

Now I can finally heal you, his wolf said with incredible relief.

Thank you. Ronan was thrilled to be back among the living—sort of. Not everything was back, however—like his memory. He was confused how he was even alive. Ronan lifted his snout and then his paws. To his delight, nothing hurt. Ronan could feel his wolf working to heal him.

When he eventually opened his eyes, he jumped up onto his paws. After a good stretch, he believed he was as good as new. The bed moved. Whoa. Blair was asleep next to him. Needing to talk to her, touch her, and love her, he shifted back into his human form.

"Blair?" His throat was so dry, the word came out a whisper.

She rolled over and faced him. "Ronan? Oh my, goddess." She reached over and clicked on the nightstand light then picked up a glass of water and handed it to him.

He guzzled half the contents. "How long have I been out?"

She sat up and ran a hand down his face almost as if she couldn't believe he was real. "Almost two weeks."

Fewer grays and more pinks poured off her. "Two weeks?" He looked down at his arms, noting that the scratches from the fight had healed. Something was amiss. He'd just shifted, and his wolf couldn't have healed him that fast. "And you? I saw Darinda toss you against the rock. How are you feeling?"

She didn't seem to have any scratches or wounds of any kind, though her bear would have healed her in two weeks' time.

"I'm good, but I've been so worried about you, that's all. Missy tried to heal you, but she only partially succeeded. We even had a shifter doctor examine you, but he too said it was up to you at that point. When you still didn't rouse, I called Ophelia. She called in a friend, and together they were able to heal you." Her words rushed out faster than a broken dam.

Ronan gathered Blair in his arm. Never had anything felt so good. "It's all so fantastic. Tell me everything that happened."

She detailed how after Ronan challenged Darinda to hand-to-hand combat, Ronan tried to slice off Darinda's head.

"I remember that much, but that's all."

"She knocked the sword from your hands, and I picked it up. Just as she turned, I lifted the sword and sliced off her head."

"You killed her?"

"Yes."

"That's amazing. What did I do during this decapitation?"

"You passed out." She explained about how she contacted Missy, Zane, and Jackson, and the men had transported him home. Blair hugged him. "Oh, Ronan. I was so scared you would die." She sniffled, and then swiped a finger under her eyes. "Darinda put a curse on you. That's why you didn't rouse."

"A curse? That explains why it took so many people to heal me."

"Yes. I still don't believe I had the guts to cut off someone's head, but she was hurting the man I love. I had to do something."

His love for Blair soared. He didn't care about the rest of the story. "You love me?"

"More than anything."

His whole body responded to her. The moment he inhaled, he realized he stunk something fierce. "I want to kiss you worse than anything, but if I don't take a shower, I'll go blind from the colors of my stench."

Blair laughed. "It's so good to hear your voice and have you back among the living." She inhaled and wrinkled her nose. "But yes, go."

"Go back to sleep. No telling how long I'll be in there."

Ronan slipped into the bathroom across the hall, closed the door, and turned on the shower. Not able to wait until the water warmed, he stepped under the flow, reveling in the feeling of being alive. The fact Blair wasn't seriously injured was even more spectacular. His biggest worry now was her state of mind. He'd killed his share of criminals, especially in his wolf form, but he'd ended a person's life only a handful of times—and that was by gunshot. He couldn't imagine the feeling of cutting off a person's head. Slicing through a watermelon wasn't the same.

The water warmed, and he soaped up, scrubbing every inch of his body. Only after he shampooed his hair and beard did he feel human again.

He'd just turned off the water and stepped out when the bathroom door opened. Blair appeared, naked and delicious, and his wolf howled. Every inch of his body tingled. He was back.

"Hello," he said as he stepped onto the mat. Her eyes widened, and her hues intensified, filling the space with lime green. "The shower's free," he announced.

"I couldn't sleep knowing you were in here naked. How do you feel? I mean, really feel? The truth."

"I'm one hundred percent." Ronan pounded his chest Tarzan style, and she laughed, just as he'd hoped.

"I wish you could have met the dragon shifter who cured you."

"Dragon shifter?"

Blair stepped past him and ducked into the shower. She turned on the water, and his cock throbbed from needing her. "His name was Declan Sinclair. He's from Tarradon, the same realm where Finn McKinnon now resides."

"I'm confused. Ophelia's friend was from another realm?" Maybe he wasn't at full speed yet.

She explained how desperate she'd become for help. "Only Ophelia had any connections. I don't know how she pulled it off, but a few days after I contacted her, she showed up at our doorstep with a giant of a man. Together, they removed the curse. You don't remember any of it?"

"No."

Blair ran the soap down her body, and Ronan could think of nothing other than mating with her once and for all. After all they had been through, there was no doubt that he and Blair were perfect for each other. She was strong, caring, and loyal. A man couldn't ask for more.

He pressed his face against the glass door. "Need any help?"

"No!" She grinned. "I'm almost finished. Are you sure there are no after effects?"

He grabbed his hard cock. "Nope. I'm rarin' to go."

Blair laughed and ducked her head under the water. "I feel better, too. Your body had healed with the help of Missy and the doctor, but your mind wouldn't let go of the darkness."

"I remember struggling to wake up and thinking something was holding me down."

"Darinda's curse."

"All I can say is good riddance to that bitch. Maybe now the dark gods and goddesses will leave us alone considering how we—or rather you—handled Darinda."

"It was mostly you—and Zane. His shield and sword lived up to the hype."

Ronan nodded. "Speaking of which, where are my weapons?"

"Zane has them."

That was for the best. "I doubt I'll have any use from them again. At least I hope I won't."

Blair rinsed her hair. When she turned off the water, he growled.

"Behave," she said. "You don't want a relapse."

After pulling open the door, she stepped onto the mat, and he handed her a towel. Blair bent over and wrapped it around her head. Once she returned upright, he took a second towel and dried her back.

"I've missed this," she said.

"Me too. I'm sorry I failed you."

She twisted around. "Failed me? How can you say that? You had to fight that horrible lookalike creature, and then battle Darinda when you could barely stand." She dragged her hands down his chest. "If anything had happened to you, I would have died— literally."

He tapped her nose, not liking how her lime greens had totally disappeared. "How about we forget Darinda now and concentrate on us?"

Blair smiled. "I'd like that." She slowly removed the towel and her long hair curled delicately around her shoulders. He lifted the towel from her fingers and tossed it over the shower door.

Ronan groaned and moved closer. He couldn't resist smelling her wet locks. The scent created a new set of colors—greens and blues—that jacked up his libido.

"Be good."

He huffed. "Not on your life."

When he slid the towel over her breasts, her nipples puckered. He then swung her up into his arms, and Blair laughed. "Be careful."

"Of?"

"Of hurting yourself. You're still weak."

"Is that so? I plan to change your mind about that fact." Ronan edged open the door with his foot and carefully carried a rather wet Blair across the hallway into their room.

While he was showering, Blair had been busy changing the

sheets for which he was thankful. After placing her on the bed, Ronan crawled next to her, admiring and thrilling at the love in her eyes. "I think it's time we made this relationship official."

"You won't get an argument from me." Blair reached up and tugged on his beard. "I love you, my sword wielding wolf."

He smiled. "I love you more."

Wanting to give her all the affection and attention she deserved, he hoped he could last. Two weeks without Blair was way too long for him and his wolf.

Once Ronan started loving her, it seemed as if his control was never as manageable as he wanted. He cradled her in his arms and kissed her. Big mistake. His cock nearly exploded, and his wolf begged for release.

Please, not now. We need to make her ours first, he said, reprimanding his wolf.

Then hurry.

Hurrying would take away from the wonder of their mating. Blair dragged her fingers through his hair, and he'd never felt so alive. Every minute with her brought him such joy.

After a thorough tongue-twisting kiss, he lifted his head. "I need to explore all of you."

"Be fast because I want to do the same to you. After all, I need to be sure you're really healed."

"Oh, I'm healthy all right—and quite ready. Just to set the record straight, I've known you were my mate long before your bear woke up."

She smiled. "Then I will give you all the credit for finding her."

After crawling on top of Blair, Ronan slid down the bed until his lips were at breast height. Even in his state of near death, he'd dreamed of tasting her again. The first suck had him soaring and his wolf rejoicing. When Blair arched her back and offered herself to him, he could barely keep from plunging into her. His desire for her knew no bounds. She was everything he could want, and he vowed to protect her until his last breath.

"Blair…," he whispered as he drew a taut peak into his mouth. His blue sparks rained down on them.

She reached up, grabbed at one, but failed at capturing the light. "I love these."

If only they were physical, he'd give her a boatload. "That's my way of showing you how much I want you."

Her nails dug into his shoulders, encouraging him.

Take her now, his wolf shouted.

This mating is about her as much as it is about us, he ground back.

"I wish I had them too," Blair answered, "so you can see how incredibly turned on I am."

He looked up and smiled. "Trust me, I can tell. Your colors are more magnificent than my blue sparks. Your greens and rose colors tell me how much you want me."

"I'm glad," she panted.

"Then let me see if I can excite you further."

"It's not possible," she whispered.

After he feasted on her breasts, he dropped lower. Her colors intensified and swirled around her. Once they mated, he hoped she would be able to experience his colorful visions too. Then she'd see what happened at the moment of their union. No light show he'd ever seen would match the array of different hues that would surround them or the spectacular range of colors when they both came together.

Ronan spread her legs, and her colors abounded. His first swipe put him so on edge, he prayed for control. Fighting for Blair and then being away from her for so long pushed him to the max.

Blair wrapped her legs around his back and clutched the sheets. Her near scream of delight had him flicking his tongue faster.

"Ronan, please. It's my turn now!"

He could never deny her anything. Blair unwrapped her legs and gently pushed him onto his back. What was about to come would surely blow his mind—assuming his cock didn't blow first.

Chapter Twenty-Two

B LAIR HAD NEVER been happier, excited, or more content in her life. Their child had lived through the ordeal with Darinda, the man she loved more than anything was alive and well, and now they would mate.

"I need to taste you too," she said.

Before Ronan had the chance to object, she rose up on her knees, leaned over, and grabbed his hard shaft.

"Wait," he called. "Stretch onto your side."

In a flash, he was twisted around so they could feast on each other at the same time. As much as she loved to receive as many licks as he could give, she found it hard to concentrate. Ronan was a master of seduction. His tongue went to work, and he then dragged the back of his hand over her hip in a slow sensual manner. The intense sensation made her fist squeeze his cock tighter. He moaned, and she pumped her hand up and down.

His tongue circled her clit, and when he drew her tiny nub deeper into his mouth, she almost forgot she'd begged to taste him. Forcing herself not to become too distracted, she drew him deep into her mouth, loving the way he tasted—so strong and clean. When she tightened her grip around his wide girth, he lifted her top leg with his elbow and drove his tongue into her opening. Pleasure pulsed. She wiggled her hips as she drew his throbbing cock deeper into her mouth.

A quick shot of cum surfaced, and she pulled back, wanting their union to be the most dynamic ever.

Blair scooted away from him. "Let me ride you."

Ronan grinned. "Climb aboard, baby."

Blair giggled.

After all they'd been through together, Ronan had become not only her fated mate, but her confidant, lover, and supporter as well. Straddling him, she leaned over and kissed his forehead, his nose, and then lightly brushed her lips against his. Ever so slowly, she lifted up, but their lips remained sealed for a moment longer.

Unable to keep apart, she reached between her legs, lifted his big cock, and placed it at her entrance. Even though she trusted her bear to prepare her, Blair had to be sure that she was ready for the final act of unifying them. She ran her tongue along her teeth and was relieved to find that they had sharpened. It was almost time.

I will never leave you again, her bear said. *I will always protect you.*

That gave her the courage she needed. When her bear roared, she plunged downward, encompassing his cock. Lustful sparks shot upward, sending mounting desire into every cell of her body.

"Oh, Ronan." Blair closed her eyes and rode him long and hard, until she was on the brink of a climax.

He grabbed her hips. "I want you to stay still as I make love to you."

Frustration bit at her until she realized that this was his way of loving her fully. "I'll try."

He eased into her and then withdrew. It felt like he was fanning the fires within, wanting to bring her to an epic climax. Needing to taste him, touch him, and smell him, she leaned over and nibbled on his ear. "I want you," she whispered.

His fingers gripped her hard, and his breaths increased. It was as if he was holding on by a thread too. She dragged her mouth down his neck, the slight salty tang elevating her unquenchable need further.

"Love me, Ronan."

His hands slid up to her waist as he dipped his head to the side of her neck. As his cock plunged into her again and again, his grunts grew louder, and his eyes turned a molten golden color. His blue aura grew and grew until both of them were entombed in his bright light. Nothing could harm them once they were mated; she was sure of it.

On the next thrust, the gates of her passion couldn't be stopped, and she pressed her mouth against his neck. She didn't know who bit who first, but the moment they were united, her world stopped spinning, and white light sped through her veins. Her climax came so powerfully that she forgot to breathe for a moment.

His hot seed shot into her, shaking her entire body, forcing her to suck in air. Blair licked her lips, tasting the slight coppery taste of blood. They both licked each other's wound to close the holes they'd made. Ronan wrapped his arms around her and held her tight, his blue glow warm and comforting.

Blair dropped her head on his shoulder and wanted to hold him forever. They must have fallen asleep because when Ronan jerked, it startled her. Lifting her head, she watched him sleep, content to never move again.

Ronan grunted a moment later then awoke. "Hi," he said as if still in a dream.

"Hi back." Blair smiled.

I've been told once we mate we can communicate with our minds. Can you understand me? he asked.

Blair had always hoped to find someone as wonderful as Ronan, but to be truly mated on such a basic level thrilled her. *Yes. I guess you'll have to watch your thoughts from now on.*

Don't worry. You'll be pleased with whatever I'm thinking, because it will always be about you.

And mine about you.

Ronan sat up, and Blair snuggled against him. "I think it's time we talk about your secret."

Blair stilled. "My secret?" He couldn't know about the baby unless Jackson had told him.

He glanced down at her stomach. "You do know that I can sense your moods, right? Your colors are very distinctive."

Just then a swirl of yellow passed in front of her eyes. She blinked, not sure if what she'd seen had been real or her imagination. "What does yellow mean?"

His brows furrowed. "Yellow?"

"I just saw a wave of color come off of you."

He grinned. "I can't believe it. I knew we might be able to communicate telepathically, but I didn't know if you'd inherit, so to speak, my ability to see scents as colors."

She grinned. "I think I can."

"I don't pay much attention to my colors as I know what I'm thinking. It should be fun for you to figure me out."

She'd liked that. "To make sure this miracle of mating wasn't a figment of my imagination, can you turn around? I want to see the marking on your shoulder." Blair wanted to keep the existence of the baby a secret a little while longer.

When she saw how her bear paw print was underneath his, her heart beat faster. She ran her fingers along the outline. "It's beautiful."

"Let me see yours." He sounded excited, which thrilled her.

She turned around, and he pressed his lips to her skin. "It's really true. We are one."

It was time to tell him the good news. She faced him again. "You're right. I do have a secret, but I didn't say anything because I was afraid I might lose the baby."

Ronan hugged her. "I can't tell you how thrilled I am. How far along are you? That's something I couldn't tell."

"About eight weeks. The shifter doctor who treated you checked me out, but I'll need to see a baby doctor soon."

He rubbed her shoulder. "You are so strong. If our baby could withstand what Darinda did to you, she'll be a marvel."

"She?"

Ronan laughed. "Or he. I don't care. I want lots of kids."

"So do I."

Blair had to be the luckiest woman in the world.

"DO YOU LIKE the sofa beneath the living room window or facing the kitchen?" Blair asked.

She still couldn't believe they were now moved into their new home. While her furniture was only enough for a one-bedroom apartment, Ronan assured her they'd fill up the rest as fast as possible.

"You're the one with the good eye," he said. "Tell me, is this the right height for this picture?"

A friend of hers from school had painted a forest scene because Blair loved the woods. "It's perfect."

For the next few hours, they arranged and rearranged the furniture. Finally, Blair had to call it quits. "How about we have some chicken wraps delivered?" she asked. "I'm too beat to cook. Besides, I'm not sure I know where everything is yet." They needed to shop soon too.

"Sounds like a great idea. You rest while I call."

"I'd like to take a shower. Moving furniture is a sweaty ordeal."

"You go head. I'll ask for a fast delivery so it will be here when you finish."

Ronan was the best, but she needed some alone time. The baby was acting up, though she couldn't blame him. When Blair decided she was having a boy, she didn't know. Her morning sickness had ended a few days ago, but it was probably because she hadn't eaten much. Her appetite had yet to return to normal.

Now that they were finally settled in their new place, she promised to take better care of herself.

Blair had just finished her shower when the doorbell rang. The deliveryman had come. Throwing on her very comfortable shorty pajamas, she padded out to the living room. "I smell food."

"Yup."

Ronan unwrapped the meal and placed it on the table, but for some reason the wraps didn't look all that appetizing. "How about we watch a movie and snuggle?" she asked.

"Sure. What kind of movie are you in the mood for?" Ronan

asked.

With an iced tea in hand, Blair moved over to the sofa and sat. "I don't care."

Ronan sat next to her and wrapped an arm around her shoulder. "Are you feeling okay?"

She smiled. "I'm fine."

"I can sense something is wrong. Your colors are duller, and I can feel some pain."

Blair didn't need an inquisition tonight. "All I need is a good night's rest, and I'll be fine." She forced a smile. "I promise."

"Okay." He leaned over and kissed her. "You better be. I need you."

Ronan was the best man ever. He even picked a romantic comedy, probably because he knew she was a big fan of love stories. Too bad she fell asleep halfway through it.

When she awoke, she was in bed and light was streaming in through the window. Thankfully, Blair was still on leave because of all that had happened. She'd told work that as soon as she moved into the house that she'd return to work. Tomorrow would be soon enough.

Pushing up on her elbows, she listened for evidence of Ronan moving about, but the house was silent. As she sat up, severe cramps attacked her. Her heart pumped hard, and she rubbed her stomach to ease the pain. "Please be okay, little one."

Once the ache subsided somewhat, she eased out of bed and made it to the living room where she'd left her purse. Ainsley would know what to do. It didn't matter that Blair had been through this before; she refused to admit that she was losing this baby too. She'd already picked out the color for the baby's room.

Another cramp tightened its hold on her, and Blair let out a small cry. This wasn't good. Not good at all. She could feel her bear trying hard to make her whole.

Chapter Twenty-Three

"THE DOCTOR WILL see you now," the nurse said.

Blair clasped Ainsley's hand. "Wish me luck."

"I hope the baby is okay."

Blair knew the baby was gone, but she wanted confirmation. The cramping, the spotting, the agony of it all had convinced her. She'd tried to keep a cheerful outlook to prevent Ronan from finding out too soon. Before he rushed to her side, she wanted the doctor to give her the official word.

Inside the exam room, the nurse told her to undress, climb on top of the table, and wait for the doctor. When the doctor finally arrived, waves of despair came crashing down on her as Blair waited for the verdict. After a few questions about her state of mind, the doctor examined her and then took some blood.

"I'll run the blood work, but I see no signs of life. I'm so sorry."

"Blair?" Ronan's voice interrupted her thoughts. It took a second for her to remember they could communicate telepathically.

"Yes?"

"I'm sensing a lot of distress. Are you okay?"

As much as she wanted to cry and tell him everything, she wasn't ready. *"Yes. I just stubbed my toe."*

The moment those words were transmitted, a new wave of depression washed over her. She hadn't wanted to lie to Ronan, but she needed more time to come to grips with what happened.

"I'm afraid we'll need to do a little procedure to clean you out," the doctor said.

"Okay, I guess."

An hour later, Blair woke from the anesthesia. She was woozy and bloated, but otherwise felt okay. Once she shifted, her bear would help her more fully recover.

"I would like you to return for a checkup in a few weeks so we can do some tests to see if there is a physical reason why you miscarried," the doctor said.

"Sure." She'd say anything. All Blair wanted was to get out of there.

Once she dressed, she barely remembered paying or riding back home in Ainsley's car.

Her friend parked in front of the new home. "I've already called into work and told them to cancel my appointments," Ainsley said. "You should not be by yourself right now."

Blair was working hard to keep it together. "You don't need to do that. I'd prefer to be alone."

Ainsley walked her up to the door and waited for Blair to unlock it. "Sorry, honey. No can do."

"I'll be fine." Those words had become her mantra. She said them now without even thinking.

"You don't sound fine. If I ever miscarried, I'd be a total basket case. I'm calling your mother."

Blair wasn't sure she could deal with her pity right now. "I'm good. Really."

"Stop saying that. This time, it isn't true. I know how much you wanted this baby, but my goddess, Blair you've been through one trauma after another. To be honest, I'm surprised the baby survived for this long."

Before she could stop her best friend, Ainsley breezed in and dialed Blair's mom. In a way, Blair was happy that Ainsley would be the one to deliver the terrible news.

Once Ainsley disconnected, she faced Blair. "She'll be right over."

Blair dropped down onto the sofa, not looking forward to this conversation. She wasn't in the mood to tell her mother this was the second baby she'd lost, but Ronan had said that if she came clean, it would clear the air between her and her family. Personally, she thought the air was clear enough.

Because their new house was in the shifter compound, her mom arrived in minutes, and Ainsley let her in. Mom rushed over and hugged her. "Oh, Blair. I am so sorry."

"So am I."

Ainsley placed a hand on Blair's shoulder. "I'll let the two of you talk, but if you need anything, and I mean anything, call me." She hugged Blair goodbye.

"Thank you for being here."

"Of course."

Once Ainsley left, Blair faced her mom. "I'm sorry."

Her mother clasped her hands. "For what? You've been through a trauma. None of this was your fault."

"Maybe, but I let my emotions get the best of me. I wasn't able to handle the stress." Her mother would have been able to handle it all. The image of Jared telling her he was already married was too much for her to bear back then. The severed head still threw her for a loop. Tears flowed.

Her mother wrapped an arm around her shoulders. "It's going to be okay. You and Ronan have plenty of time to try again."

Blair understood that her mom was trying to be helpful, but somehow it wasn't what she wanted to hear right now. She lifted her head, tears blurring her vision. "How do you know? This is the second baby I've lost. Maybe it's just me."

Blair hadn't meant to blurt that out, but all the hurt and anguish poured out of her.

"Two babies?"

Now her mother would find out what a terrible daughter she'd been, keeping something like this a secret. "It's a long story."

"I'm not going anywhere."

Blair swiped the tears from her cheeks. "Fine. I've wanted to tell you for so long, but just couldn't."

"Oh, Blair—you can always tell me anything."

She sniffled. "It was the beginning of my senior year in college when I met a man that I wanted to believe was my mate."

"Your mate, but how could that be?"

For the next half hour, Blair told her mother about the affair and why she'd kept it a secret. "By the time I found out Jared was really married and just stringing me along, I was two months pregnant. The doctors said there was no reason why I lost the baby—that it happens sometimes—but the high amount of stress and anxiety I had been dealing with probably factored in as well."

Her mom grasped her hand. "I'm not sure I can understand how you thought he was your mate, but I'll let you in on a little secret."

By now, Blair was shaking. The retelling of the story made what happened today all the more real. "What's that?"

"Before I had Kalan, I miscarried a baby girl."

Why that helped soothe her ache she didn't know. "I never knew."

"You didn't need to. As hard as it was, I got through it. Then, after Kalan was born, I miscarried again. Trust me—it was just as horrifying as the loss of the first baby. After that, thankfully it was smooth sailing."

"How did Dad react?" Guilt swamped her for not calling Ronan right away. He'd lost his baby too.

"He was even more upset, but together we survived."

Blair leaned back against the sofa. "Ronan will be devastated, too. He might appear to be this hard-boiled wolf, but deep inside, he's a softie. His family life, as you can imagine, had a lot of ups and downs, and he dreams of the white picket fence and the two point five kids worse than anyone."

Her mom rubbed her arm. "You'll get there. You just need to keep the faith."

The front door bell rang, and her mom rose. "That must be Izzy and Missy. I called them."

"Mo-om."

"You don't need to be alone right now; in fact, the more the merrier."

What was she thinking? "This isn't a party!"

Both of her friends rushed in, sympathy filling their eyes. Missy had a bag slung over her shoulder, probably to help with the healing process. They both talked at once. Her bear must have decided that she needed to take over, because one minute Blair was hugging Missy, and the next, she'd shifted.

What the hell?

"Blair?" her mother said.

She tried to shift back, but her bear prevented her. As if she had no control of anything, her bear headed for the front door, knocking over a lamp and then a vase that was a gift from her parents.

Stop this at once, she commanded her rogue bear.

"Blair, what are you doing?" her mother asked.

If she could, she'd have told her. When Blair tried to turn the knob, her big bear paws couldn't hold tight.

"Do you want to get out?" Izzy asked.

Blair's bear kicked the door.

"Open it for her," her mother said, worry filling her voice.

Izzy edged toward the door and yanked it open. As soon as she pulled it wide, Blair dashed out.

"Blair, what's wrong?" Ronan said in her head.

It was time to tell him. She tried to answer, but her thoughts came out jumbled. What was happening to her? Was this another curse put there by Darinda? Wasn't the goddess dead?

I need to protect you, her bear said. *I won't fail you again.*

Blair wanted to explain that she didn't need protection. She needed Ronan's arms wrapped around her.

Before she had the chance to stop her wild animal, they barreled toward the woods. While Blair had grown up around there, things had changed. The trees were taller and more trails existed.

Can we please stop? she begged. *I don't feel well.*

We need to hide. I have to protect you.

This is insane. No animal ever took over a shifter's body. It was like some virus, or alien creature had invaded every cell and was out of control. Just her luck to have an animal that had lain dormant for years and then suddenly go crazy.

Blair tried to shift again, but nothing she tried worked. *Why are you doing this to me?*

We'll be there soon, her animal responded, clearly not interested in what Blair wanted or needed.

"Ronan, can you hear me? I need you to find me."

He can't hear you, her bear said.

Even if that were true, Ronan would find a way to save her. Oh, why did she have to inherit this bear? Stupid animal.

I heard that, her bear responded.

She didn't care. *Please, let's stop and go back.*

The bear ignored her and continued to plow through the forest, sometimes keeping to the paths and at other times damaging the undergrowth. She marched through the tree branches as if they were butter, and stepped on rocks and fallen logs without care. A swarm of angry bees flew out from under the log and gave chase. Blair batted them away, but that only provoked them further. A few stung her. Seemingly satisfied for having inflicted harm, the bees eventually left.

A small creek appeared, and all Blair wanted to do was have a drink and rest. This time, her animal must have sensed her distress and finally stopped. Blair lowered her head and drank her fill.

While she wanted to argue with the obstinate animal, she figured it wouldn't do any good.

"Ronan, where are you? Help me."

Don't you listen? He can't hear you. I cut you off.

This was her worse nightmare. *Why?*

You need time to heal—or rather I need time to heal you. Your mom and your friends would never have left you alone. I needed to interfere.

I could have handled them.

Growing up, her bear had chastised her for rationalizing. Now her animal was doing the same thing. After another few minutes of plowing through the woods, her bear's words sunk in. Maybe she was right. Blair hadn't wanted to hear all of their kind words of sympathy. Her body and mind needed to heal first. Maybe her bear was helping. *Thank you. I think.*

You're welcome.

Her bear was on the move again, but when Blair looked around, she truly had no idea where they were. She just hoped her bear would stop soon. They crossed a meadow before coming to a set of rocks that jutted up from the earth. Her bear slowed and then wedged her hefty body between them.

Now, we rest, her bear said as she sprawled out on the ground.

Hallelujah!

Chapter Twenty-Four

I F BOTH CONNOR and Jackson hadn't been on a job, Ronan would have asked them if one of them could check on Blair. Something was wrong. The first time Ronan made contact, Blair said she was fine, but given the pain he was experiencing, she wasn't. He decided to respect her wishes. If she didn't want to tell him what was wrong, it was her choice, but he needed to let her know how much it pained him when she held back.

A few more waves of despair had hit him throughout the day, which was why he had reached out telepathically. When she didn't answer, he figured she didn't want to speak to him for some reason, or else their new telepathic abilities weren't well formed yet. Then something sharp pressed against his heart, and he decided this was more than just Blair wanting to keep something secret.

Ronan was sitting in his Jeep outside of a woman's house, waiting for the man who was accused of infidelity to leave. He'd been inside for a little more than an hour, and all during that time, Ronan's thoughts kept shooting to Blair.

Ronan had taken pictures of Deidre's husband going into the house as well as her husband's car in the drive, so he figured he didn't really need to see this guy exit. While this didn't prove they were having an affair, he was one step closer to sealing the deal. Next time, he'd move in closer and hope to get a shot inside the bedroom.

It was time to leave. On the way to his house, he called Connor and explained that he needed to leave his surveillance early.

"No problem. Definitely check on Blair. I'm worried about her too. She's been through an ordeal I wouldn't wish on anyone."

Cutting off a person's head would rank up there as high trauma. Ronan had the best boss. Blair's car was in the drive when he arrived, implying she was inside and he dashed in. "Blair?"

He didn't sense her nor did she answer. His wolf growled. Ronan headed straight to the bedroom thinking she might be ill, and her bear signature was too weak to detect. The bed was empty. What the hell?

As he returned to the living room, he noticed the vase her parents had given them as a housewarming present was missing from the table next to the door, and his gut soured.

Before he could figure out his next move, his cell rang. It was Blair's mom, and his heart dropped to his stomach. "Celia?"

"Oh, Ronan. I'm so worried about Blair." Her voice shook.

"Calm down. Tell me what happened."

"Blair lost the baby, and she was so upset that she shifted right in the house. She knocked over things and charged outside. I've tried calling her, but apparently she still isn't home."

"No, she's not." He was still stuck on the words: *she lost the baby.* "Wait a minute. Blair miscarried?"

"Yes. She was beside herself with grief. I am so sorry, Ronan. You lost a child too."

His wolf whined and scratched his insides, while Ronan's whole body became incased in lead.

"She should have called me right away." Pain sliced at him that was as brutal as when Nanor had clawed at him. "When did this happen?"

"She ran out of the house about two hours ago. Blair had just come back from her doctor's appointment."

His heart squeezed tight. Knowing his mate, Blair probably needed time to come to grips with the loss. "Don't worry. I'll find her."

"Be gentle when you do. This is a terrible blow to her. She

knows how much you wanted a child."

Blair shouldn't be worried about him at a time like this. "I'll let you know when I have her."

Ronan would find Blair. He wasn't a bounty hunter for nothing. His tracking skills were unparalleled because of his ability to see scents as colors. He dashed into the bedroom and located his wolf backpack. He filled it with a pair of lightweight nylon shorts and sandals for himself for when he shifted back into his human form, and then tossed in a pair of panties, shorts, and sandals for Blair. He had to tie the T-shirt to the outside, as the pack was full already. Blair could wear one of his shirts. It would cover her more. He just hoped she was able to walk.

What he couldn't understand was why didn't she answer him when he'd called out to her? Was she injured? His gut churned at that horrible idea.

Hurry, his wolf urged.

While Ronan was a good tracker in human form, he was exceptional as a wolf. He undressed and then stepped outside with his pack. After closing the door, he shifted. He had putting on the pack down to a science. Nudging his nose under the strap, he held down one side with his paw, and slithered underneath. While he couldn't close the clasp under his chest, he could run with it on and not lose it.

Ronan took off and immediately sensed Blair's colors, but they were only thin wisps in the air. Had he not been mated with her, he might have confused the grays with that of the cloudy sky. Her mother had said she had headed toward the woods, and the colors confirmed that.

Once he reached the edge of the forest, he took the path, but it wasn't long before a wide swath of broken branches led him in a different direction.

"Blair, can you hear me?" he telepathed.

Damn, why wasn't she answering? He wasn't experiencing any pain from her, but that didn't mean she wasn't hurt. Her bear could be working hard to keep her alive.

Frustrated, Ronan pushed harder into the woods, keeping an open mind about where the bear might have gone. Given the crushed underbrush, staying on the trail hadn't been her concern.

When he neared a stream, Blair's pinks and purples abounded, and he left out a breath. While he looked around, absorbing the earth's colors, he drank the water. Once across the stream, he came to a meadow full of wild flowers, but there the scent seemed to disappear.

Ronan howled, hoping his mate would respond. She wasn't close or he would have sensed it.

A long line of trees edged the meadow. *"Tell me where you are, Blair. Please. I know you're upset, but so am I."*

A hint of pink floated to the north, and Ronan followed the color. What made him turn toward the collection of tall boulders, he didn't know, but when he spotted Blair asleep on the ground, he nearly howled with joy.

Wanting to be in his human form, he rolled onto his back, slipped out of his backpack, and then shifted. If she didn't respond to his telepathy, perhaps she'd wake with the sound of his voice. Once he slipped on his shorts and sandals, he carried over the pack to where she was resting and knelt next to her. "Blair?"

No response. Damn.

Needing to be closer to her, he lay behind her and curled his body around her back. Ronan stroked her fur from her head to her hip, hoping his scent and warmth would calm her. "Blair, can you hear me?" While she didn't move, a low growl escaped. He hoped it wasn't a warning to keep away. He wouldn't obey that request. "I'm sorry about the baby, but I'm here for you. We'll work through this, I promise. When the time is right, we'll have another child."

One of Blair's paws moved, and she started to roll over on him.

Moving fast, Ronan scooted out of the way and then jumped to his feet. When her eyes opened, he smiled. "Hi. Can you shift for me?" he asked.

Her bear rolled back over, as if she wanted nothing to do with him. What was that about? "I'm just as torn up about the baby as you are," he said.

Or was that not what she wanted to hear? Blair was proud and was the type to suffer in silence. *Think.* There had to be something to bring her out of her funk.

Ronan sat back down, leaned against a rock, and stretched out his legs, pretending he was back in their living room with his feet propped up on the coffee table. "So, I was hired by a woman to follow her husband to see if he was cheating. That was where I was all day."

If she didn't want to discuss the loss, he could talk about his work. Blair was always asking him about his job. He waited to see if she stirred, but she didn't. Her breathing however increased, implying she was awake.

"Did I catch him, you might ask? Well, I have photos of him going into this woman's home, but they could have been just watching a movie. Crazy, you say? Maybe. Tomorrow, I'll go back and see if he sneaks into her place again. You want to hear another story? Because no matter what, I'm not leaving you, even if I have to stay out here all night." Nothing. "Listen, Blair. I love you. I'll always love you more than anything."

Her bear rolled over and sat up. When she reached out a paw, Ronan offered his hand, waiting to see what she would do. Blair's bear stood and Ronan did too. Then fur flew and legs waved. A second later, his beautiful mate was naked in front of him. He was smart enough not to ask if she was okay. Blair would just say yes.

Instead, he held out his arms and waited for her to come to him. Tears streaming down her cheeks, she edged toward him.

"You found me," she said then sniffled.

"Your colors are bright." He wouldn't mention all the grays and dark blues he spotted, signaling intense depression.

"I see some blues and greens coming off you, as well as orange," she said.

"The orange is left over from when I was scared shitless that I'd lost you."

Blair stepped into his embrace, and every trace of orange disappeared. Blair was safe now, and he would keep her that way forever. He ran his hands down her back, loving the curve of her spine. She was the bravest woman he'd ever met—mate or no mate.

"I was scared too," she said. "My bear wouldn't let me go. She wanted to protect and cure me."

Now wasn't the time to discuss what curing her meant, but he was glad she was feeling better. He kissed her forehead, wanting her to decide how much loving she wanted. "Is anyone hungry?" he asked.

A small smile lifted her lips. "Would it be too clichéd to say, I'm hungry as a bear?"

Ronan hadn't meant to laugh, but he couldn't help it. "Absolutely not. I'm thinking about a big piece of red meat at the Lake Steakhouse. You up for it?"

"Can I go naked?"

He adored her sense of humor. "Absolutely not. I'm the only one to enjoy that pleasure." He picked up his pack. "I brought you some clothes. I would have grabbed more, but it was all I could fit into the pack. Wolves don't make good pack mules."

"I'm thrilled you brought anything." He handed her the clothing, and she pulled them on. "Perfect."

Hand in hand, they headed back. Blair didn't seem to be in a big hurry, and he was fine with that. As much as he wanted to ask what prompted her to shift, when she was ready, she'd tell him. Right now, she needed him to listen and give her all of his support.

BLAIR COULDN'T BELIEVE how good she felt physically. Yes, she was distraught over the loss of her child, but having a few hours to think things through while her bear healed her from the inside and then protected her from everything and everyone had helped. When she'd opened her eyes and saw Ronan there, she knew things would be okay—for real this time. Would she mourn this baby's death? Absolutely, but it wouldn't be fair to Ronan if she didn't try to move on.

He was her hero. On the way home, he didn't even ask her any questions or bug her about why she didn't respond to his calls. He'd stated that her mother had told him everything, and that she could take all the time she needed to sort things through. Just having him by her side brought her such relief.

When they returned home, they showered together, touching each other ever so gently. Ronan's colors were subdued, and Blair assumed hers were too. Now more than ever, she wanted to be with him intimately, but her body would tell her when she was ready.

After they dried off, Blair told him she wanted to call her mother so she wouldn't worry. For once, she didn't dread the conversation, because Blair planned to be brutally honest.

Ronan followed her out. "Would you like a glass of wine before we head to dinner?"

"I'd love a glass." Tonight would be a sort of celebration—of the life that was lost and of the two lives that were starting fresh without the threat of death hanging over their heads.

She dialed her mother and wasn't disappointed when her mom asked if she was okay. "Not completely. I have a lot to process, but Ronan is here to help."

"Oh, sweetheart, I am so happy for you. Were you able to get your bear under control?"

"Eventually."

"When you were young, you struggled with her so much."

She had? How had she blocked out those memories? "Ronan helped me. My bear was so humiliated for abandoning me after I met Jared that she wanted to make it up to me by protecting me against the onslaught of concern. While I told her I appreciated her attempt to keep me safe, her methods weren't the best."

Her mother chuckled. "Oh, Blair. You are so right."

"I'm afraid I have to go. Ronan and I are going to dinner. We'll catch up later."

"Just remember I love you, no matter what you do," her mother said. "Your dad and I are so very proud of you."

Those words brought tears to her eyes. "I love you back."

Ronan placed a comforting hand on her back and handed her a glass of wine as soon as she hung up.

"How did it go?" he asked.

"Good. Being honest with my mom brought us closer." She sipped her wine, and the liquid soothed her throat. "Perfect."

"I'm glad things worked out."

"Me too."

They talked about when she planned to go back to work, and then how he planned to catch that woman's husband in the act, so to speak.

Ronan lifted the empty glass from her fingers. "Ready for dinner?"

"Yes."

Ronan set down the glasses, picked her up, and spun her around. "Did I tell you how incredibly happy you make me?"

"No. You've been unconscious for much of our courtship, remember?" She was teasing of course, but Ronan was an easy one to do that to.

"I think my memory must have been erased."

They both laughed then headed out to dinner.

Chapter Twenty-Five

Five months later

BLAIR HELD UP two dresses. "Which looks better—the pink one or the green one?"

Vinea and her new baby, Emma—named after her best friend EmmaLee—had come to town to show Devon's parents their new grandchild. Because Vinea hadn't been down since her last visit, Blair wanted to help host a baby shower for her.

"The green one," Ronan said. "It complements your gorgeous auburn hair better."

"Then green it is." Just as she was about to put it on, Ronan slipped it from her fingers. "What are you doing?" she asked, as if she couldn't guess from the color change in his eyes or the fact his beard had grown thicker. Blair just loved whenever he told her what he planned to do to her.

"What do you think?" he asked with that adorable smile of his that she never could resist.

She dragged a finger down his chest. "We have a party to attend."

"So?" Ronan drew her into his arms and kissed her, making her forget about everyone but the two of them. These last five months had been full of laughter, joy, and deep exploration that she never wanted to end.

He stepped back and removed his briefs. Now naked, he slipped his hands behind her back and unhooked her bra. "I think these should be banned. Maybe we should make a new rule in the house."

She chuckled. "What's that?"

"We have to walk around naked."

"If we did that, we'd never eat, the house would be a mess, and I dare say we'd both be fired for not showing up to work."

He laughed. "The real question is do I care?"

As if this conversation was now ended, he leaned over and sucked on her breast. Sparks flew from both of them, and the tiny blue bursts never ceased to amaze her. Ronan's deft tongue twirled and plucked, pushing her higher. She'd been told her need for Ronan would lessen with time, but so far, it had only escalated. During her breaks at work, she'd often rush over to McKinnon and Associates and *enjoy* Ronan. Twice her boss had questioned her, but she gave some excuse about where she was, followed by a promise to work a few Saturdays to make up the time.

Blair threaded her fingers through his hair, the silky texture altering something inside her. Everything about Ronan excited her more and more each day.

"Only because we have to make an appearance at the party will I hurry," Ronan said as he swept her up in his arms.

Blair laughed. "You are so full of shit. You can't wait any more than I can."

"So true."

He placed her on the bed then crawled on top. Ronan nibbled on her lips, then her chin, and finally that special spot on her neck that he loved to bite. Heat speared her as her desire ratcheted higher.

Blair reached between their bodies and grabbed his cock. Ronan groaned. He then captured her lips, sending a current straight between her legs. She delved into the wet heat of his mouth, which stirred her feral needs, and the rough scratch of his beard only added to the thrill of the kiss.

Cupping her face, he thrust his tongue deeper into her mouth, and she wrapped her legs around his waist. Her anticipation soared. Their breaths mingled, and their colors blended. Between their blue

Wendayan glow and their colorful scents, the room became a kaleidoscope of marvel. She bet the Aurora Borealis couldn't compete in intensity or beauty.

"Oh, Ronan," she moaned once she came up for air. Her mate was so much more than she had ever thought he could be.

"I have to taste more of you," Ronan panted as he slipped between her thighs, her legs falling to each side.

Not only did he dip two fingers into her opening, he flicked his tongue across her sensitive nub, causing a torrent of ecstasy to swamp her. She clutched his shoulders and tried not to dig her nails into him too deeply. "Yes."

Each lick and suck built her heat until she was filled with excruciating pleasure. Blair wasn't sure if she could last.

"Come for me, my little bear."

His nickname for her almost made her laugh since her bear was anything but little. When he wiggled his fingers and pressed on her most sensitive spot, she let out a gasp, her climax marching in and stealing her breath.

As the waves of erotic lust washed over her, she released her hold on him. Wanting to tease him back, she sagged. "Thank you. Now we can get dressed and go."

His eyes swirled with dark browns, and his scent turned light blue. "I know your game, my love."

Blair tried to act all innocent. "And what's that?"

"You are awash in lime green with highlights of pinks and purples. Your need for me has only escalated, not diminished."

"Is that so? What are you going to do about it?" She loved when he talked dirty to her.

Ronan leaned over and pressed his lips to her ear. "Why I'm going to fuck you, my little bear. I'm going to move so slowly that you will beg me to take you fully."

Blair couldn't help but laugh. Ronan had a hair trigger. Much to his dismay, he often came quicker than planned. "I dare you to last that long."

"I'm going to try. Hold on for the ride of your life."

Blair grabbed the back of his head, pulled his face to hers, and kissed like there was no tomorrow. When Ronan clutched a handful of her hair, she nearly lost it again. As he circled his tongue around hers, her moans grew louder. It was almost as if he was trying to mate the two together.

On instinct, Blair planted her feet on the mattress and squeezed her knees against his hips. A second later, his cock found its destination. Deliciously wicked flames crawled up her spine, electrifying her with a heightened passion. His big dick stretched her wide, but the slight initial ache made their lovemaking that much more satisfying.

Arching her back for more contact with his wonderfully muscled chest, she held on tight, as he drove into her over and over again. Each thrust made her quiver with such carnal joy that she wanted to scream.

Ronan broke the kiss and slid his lips to her neck. It was his signal that he was on the edge of coming. She too could barely hold on. The loving was so incredible that she was about to burst.

Just as she brought her own lips to his neck and inhaled, their blue orbs encased each other. Colors flowed, darting in and around them until she was nearly blinded with the glory.

When they both clamped down on each other's neck, the flood-gates broke. Just as his hot cum seared her, her release shattered. Their minds seemed to meld together, and their heartbeats became one.

Love surrounded them—for eternity.

They held on tightly until their bodies regained their strength. Ronan planted little kisses on her cheek and then her lips, his love reigniting her. Far quicker than she wanted, Ronan uncoupled. "Time to go."

She moaned. "Hold me one more minute?"

"Okay, but I make no promises to be good."

She smiled. "I hope you won't be."

THE SEX HAD been so intense that Blair was a little unsteady when she and Ronan arrived at the party.

Unsure of what Vinea needed for her newborn, Blair had picked out a cute dress for Emma. While the goddess probably could make all of the baby clothes with a swipe of a hand, she claimed she was trying to be as human as possible.

No surprise, the party was in full swing when they arrived. The house had a few holiday decorations left over from Christmas, but the added balloons and congratulation signs were a nice added touch.

A group of family and friends was huddled around Vinea and the baby, and Blair couldn't help but check out the new arrival.

EmmaLee was standing next to Vinea, holding her namesake, beaming down at the baby. While Vinea hadn't inherited Devon's ability to shift, Blair wondered if the baby would be able to. Perhaps more importantly, would the baby be a goddess?

Vinea looked up and smiled. "You made it."

"I wouldn't miss it for the world." Especially since she'd helped organize the affair. Blair set her present down on the coffee table that was already laden with gifts.

Vinea stepped around the baby admirers and hugged her. "I still can't believe you bested Darinda. Thank you."

"I can't believe I did it either, but if I hadn't, we wouldn't be here. In a way, Darinda caused her own downfall. If she hadn't turned her back on me and ignored me, I wouldn't have been able to grab the sword."

"Darinda's biggest flaw always was her arrogance. She believed she was invincible. The last laugh is on her."

They chatted a bit more when suddenly a hush spread over the crowd, and Vinea's gaze shifted to behind Blair. Her mouth opened, and it looked as if Vinea was actually shaking.

"Naliana? Mother? Father?" The door opened, and James, Naliana's immortal husband, walked in last.

Devon rushed to Vinea's side and wrapped an arm around her

waist to hold her up.

Vinea's sister floated closer. "You don't think we would stay away now, did you? I just had to hold my niece."

Vinea's mom neared. "And all I want is to hold my only grand-daughter."

Vinea planted a hand on her hip. "She's staying here on earth."

Her mother smiled. "I would never consider separating a mother from her daughter." She glanced over at her husband. "It is the worst pain anyone can ever experience."

Blair glanced at Vinea, whose mouth was still open. As if in a spell, she gathered the bundled baby from EmmaLee and handed her daughter to her mother. "I can't tell you how much those words mean to me. To be honest, I never thought I'd see you again."

Blair had never met Vinea's parents or her sister, because they lived in an entirely different realm. Her dad stepped forward. "We won't be strangers anymore. How about a hug for your old man?"

Vinea's arms still shook, and her breathing came out fast as she stepped into her father's embrace. Even Blair was on the verge of crying at the awesome reunion. Vinea had been cast out of the light realm hundreds of years ago and had suffered greatly during that time. How wonderful for her parents to forgive her and for Vinea to look kindly on her dad once more.

Her dad leaned back. "Aren't you going to introduce us to the man you gave up your immortality for? He must be pretty special."

Naliana spoke up. "He's more than special, Dad, since I picked him out for my dear sister."

While Vinea made the introductions, Ronan moved next to Blair and wrapped his arm around her shoulder, sending warmth throughout her body. She looked up at him. "When we have a baby, I bet your mother will be there in spirit."

"I'm sure she will be." He tightened his grip. "Lexi will make a great aunt too."

"That she will."

Blair placed a hand on her stomach. When she returned from the party, she planned on doing a pregnancy test, hoping for the best.

Blair's parents ambled over. "You're looking a little flushed, Blair," her mother said.

"The truth? I'm just thinking about what it will be like to have a child of our own. If we do, you just have to promise me you won't spoil your grandchild like I have a feeling Vinea's parents will do to her child."

"Do we spoil Kalan's children?"

"Totally."

Her mom grinned. "Then we will spoil yours just as much."

Hopefully, Ronan could help rein them in. Though knowing her mate, he'd be the worst culprit, and Blair couldn't be happier.

I hope you enjoyed Ronan and Blair's story. While I am ending this series, the characters in the spinoff series, Hidden Realms of Silver Lake, will be returning here. So stay tuned.

Note that Finn McKinnon is the hero in book one [Awakened By Flames], and his twin Chelsea is the heroine of book four [Destiny in Flames].

Don't forget to sign up for my newsletter to receive three free books, as well as up-to-date information on my stories. If you prefer to only receive notices regarding my releases, follow me on BookBub.

HIDDEN REALMS OF SILVER LAKE (Paranormal)

Awakened By Flames (book 1)

Seduced By Flames (book 2)

Kissed By Flames (book 3)

Destiny In Flames (book 4)

WERES & WITCHES OF SILVER LAKE

A Magical Shift (book 1) – FREE

Catching Her Bear (book 2)

A Surge of Magic (book 3)

The Bear's Forbidden Wolf (book 4)

Her Reluctant Bear (book 5)

Freeing His Tiger (book 6)

Protecting His Wolf (book 7)

Waking His Bear (book 8)

Melting Her Wolf's Heart (book 9)

Her Wolf's Guarded Heart (book 10)

His Rogue Bear (book 11)

PACK WARS (Paranormal)

Training Their Mate (book 1)

Claiming Their Mate (book 2)

Rescuing Their Virgin Mate (book 3)

Loving Their Vixen Mate (book 4)

Fighting For Their Mate (book 5)

Enticing Their Mate (book 6)

Boxed Set (books 1-3)

Boxed Set (books 1-4)

Complete Box Set (books 1–6)

MONTANA PROMISES (Full length contemporary)
Promises of Mercy (book 1)
Foundations For Three (book 2)
Montana Fire (book 3)
Hart To Hart (book 4)
Burning Seduction (book 5)
Montana Promises Complete Box Set (books 1–5)

ROCK HARD, MONTANA (contemporary novellas)
Montana Desire (book 1)
Awakening Passions (book 2)

PLEDGED TO PROTECT (contemporary romantic suspense)
Panic and Passion (book 1)
Danger and Desire (book 2)
Terror and Temptation (book 3)
Pledged To Protect Box Set (books 1–3)

HIDDEN HILLS SHIFTERS (Paranormal)
An Unexpected Diversion (book 1) – FREE
Bare Instincts (book 2)
Shifting Destinies (book 3)
Box Set (books 1–3)
Embracing Fate (book 4)
Promises Unbroken (book 5)

A NASH MYSTERY (Contemporary)
Sidearms and Silk (book 1)
Black Ops and Lingerie (book 2)

Author Bio

Want 3 FREE books? Sign up for my newsletter.

COPY AND PASTE INTO YOUR BROWSER:
smarturl.it/o4cz93?IQid=MLite

Check out my latest interview on You Tube:
youtube.com/watch?v=sQo5pyyVMDI

Not only do I love to read, write, and dream, I'm an extrovert. I enjoy being around people and am always trying to understand what makes them tick. Not only must my books have a happily ever after, I need characters I can relate to. My men are wonderful, dynamic, smart, strong, and the best lovers in the world (of course).

I believe I am the luckiest woman. I do what I love and I have a wonderful, supportive husband, who happens to be hot!

Fun facts about me

(1) I'm a math nerd who loves spreadsheets. Give me numbers and I'll find a pattern.
(2) I love photography, so I'll be posting pictures—especially of my Costa Rican adventure.
(3) I also like to exercise. Yes, I know I'm odd. Not only do I lift weights, I love to hike and walk on the beach (yes, it sounds like an ad for a date).

I love hearing from readers either on FB or via email (hint, hint).

Social Media Sites

Website:
www.velladay.com

FB:
facebook.com/vella.day.90

Twitter:
@velladay4

Gmail:
velladayauthor@gmail.com

Google:
plus.google.com/u/0/116041077486216602121/posts

Instagram:
@dayvella

www.ingramcontent.com/pod-product-compliance
Lightning Source LLC
Chambersburg PA
CBHW022059170626
46808CB00002B/511